MAISIE AT 8000 FEET

or

The Places We Let Go

MAISIE AT 8000 FEET

or

The Places We Let Go

❧

Frederick Reuss

UNBRIDLED BOOKS

Unbridled Books

Bird's Eye View of Egg Harbor City, N.J. F. Scheu, 1865. Library of Congress Geography and Map Division; *Aero view of Egg Harbor City*, New Jersey. Hughes & Cinquin, c1924. Library of Congress Geography and Map Division; *Gateway at Labnah from Views of Ancient Monuments in Central America and Yucatan* from Library of Congress Prints and Photographs Division.

All original artwork by Patrick Basse used in the creation of this book is used by permission. All rights to this artwork are reserved.

Reuss, Frederick, 1960-
Maisie at 8000 feet : a novel / Frederick Reuss.
pages ; cm
ISBN 978-1-60953-128-7 (pbk. : alk. paper)
ISBN 978-1-60953-129-4 (ebook)
I. Title. II. Title: Maisie at eight thousand feet.
PS3568.E7818M35 2016
813'.54--dc23
2015022967

1 3 5 7 9 10 8 6 4 2

Book Design by SH · CV

First Printing

For Robin and Tamie

I am the world in which I walk.

· WALLACE STEVENS ·

one

Maisie was over the Hackensack River when a Pan Am Boeing 707 passed less than a thousand feet above her. She dipped her shoulder and banked to the left, away from the flight path of the big jet coming out of Newark, then turned south, keeping the orange ribbon that was the New Jersey Turnpike to her right and the vast blackness of the Atlantic on the left horizon. It was cold. She passed through gauzy wisps of cloud and tucked her head into her collar as she passed over the port of Elizabeth, stinkier than usual—a confetti of sparkling points sprawling below.

She followed the line of trucks and cars streaming beneath her in a narrow jet of red taillights flowing south, then branching westward toward Philly and eastward toward the Jersey Shore. It reminded her of the diagram of the human circulatory system that hung in her classroom at school—the place where the two external iliac veins in the legs come together and enter the common vein in the trunk of the body—except that the nighttime roadway was just a formless arcade of light, which made her wonder about each individual car and truck, where they were coming from, where they were going, and exploded the whole picture into a dimension she had trouble imagining.

Maisie slowed and came down quickly, swooping over power lines and landing with a hop and a skip at the far end of the parking lot. The rapid descent made her feel a little queasy and light-headed. She pinched her nostrils and blew to equalize the pressure in her ears. Service areas were the safest landing places along the turnpike. Flat, open to the sky. Alden's green-and-white Volkswagen Westfalia was parked in a patch of darkness by the fence. Duchamp the camper, he called it. Duchamp had a pop top and louvered windows and a sink and an ice box and curtains you could close for privacy. She climbed in and shut the door behind her. Where's Boris? she asked herself. The raccoon's cage was empty. Maybe Alden had let him go. Maisie checked the water and food in his bowl and climbed into the front seat. They'd found Boris at the side of the turnpike a few days earlier. His rear leg had been injured, probably hit by a car. They made a cage for him out of a food crate, fed and took care of him, and now he was nearly recovered. He seemed grateful to them but, even so, was always a little nervous and trembly. All it took was a screech of tires or the hiss of air brakes or a slamming door to turn the inside of the camper into a tangle of claws and fur. Getting the frightened raccoon back into his box was no picnic.

Duchamp smelled strongly of food scraps and damp fur. Maisie sank into the passenger seat and looked up into the pop top at the fluorescent star decals Alden had stuck there. Raccoons are nocturnal animals, and Alden said seeing the stars up there probably calmed them. Alden was a Piney. He was used to living outdoors and being around wild animals and could as easily have skinned and worn Boris on his head as set his broken paw and taken him for walks on a leash. There was a little grassy area along the back fence with picnic tables. An eight-year-old girl could do just about anything she felt like in all the coming and going there, including care for an injured raccoon, and not be noticed. Maisie watched in the side mirror as a big truck backed into one of the parking spaces with loud squeaks and squeals, then finally shuddered and came to a stop. The driver hopped from the cab, lit a cigarette, and stood smoking in front of the enormous grill of his rig. Maisie put her feet up on Duchamp's dashboard and slid down into the seat. She liked feeling tucked in behind panels and glass and hinges, with dials to look at and mirrors to watch from. She imagined it was what the cockpit of an airplane felt like. She'd never sat in the cockpit of an airplane, but she felt a kinship with pilots and wondered how well, given her natural flying ability, she would manage at the controls of a big machine, if she would take to it at all or only feel unnatural, like a fish captaining a submarine or a tortoise driving a tank.

Alden startled her awake. He was holding Boris in his arms and struggling with the door handle. "That's a good boy," he said to the squirming raccoon. "Found him by the Dumpster eating French fries."

Maisie scooted out of the way as Alden pushed the struggling animal into the crate and closed the top. "How'd he get loose?"

Alden slammed the door without answering. A second later he was behind the wheel, starting the engine.

"What's wrong? Why are we leaving?" Maisie crawled forward as Alden backed out of the parking space. She slid into the front seat and glanced back to make sure the crate was still closed. "Why are we leaving?" she asked again, looking out the window as Alden shifted gears and punched the accelerator. They merged with a rattle into turnpike traffic. He glanced at her in the way he had of outlining the full meaning of a thing without speaking, then reached into his shirt pocket and took out an envelope. "Count it," he said and handed it to her. When she told him how much was there he said, "Count it again." When it came out the same he shook his head and drove for a while without saying anything. He pulled off at the next service area, told Maisie to wait, and went inside.

"You need to use the bathroom?" he asked when he returned a little while later.

Maisie shook her head. "Where are we going?"

"To let Boris go."

"Think he's ready?"

"Ready as he'll ever be."

When they were back on the highway he said, "We shouldn't have started treating him like a pet."

"He was hurt."

"Yes. But he's still wild." Alden looked at Maisie and smiled.

Half an hour later they were on a dark highway that ran flat and straight and soon gave way to forest. Maisie was about to ask where they were going when Alden put on the brakes and rolled to a stop in the middle of the road. He backed up about a hundred feet and drove straight into the woods through a narrow cut in the trees. The headlights cast an arc of light that dissolved quickly and formed a tunnel of green and brown and black. Slowly they drove deeper into the forest. The ground was soft and sandy beneath the tires. Branches scraped the sides and the roof. Maisie was too excited and too scared to ask where they were going. Her heart began to race. She could tell by the way Alden leaned forward and gripped the steering wheel that he knew exactly where they were. All at once they broke into a clearing. He turned off the lights and cut the engine. The sudden shock of total darkness took Maisie's breath away. "Let your eyes adjust," Alden said. "Just takes a few minutes."

It was very quiet. Gradually the darkness yielded and another world began to emerge. When Alden rolled down his window a torrent of sounds and fragrances rushed in. Maisie could make out blotted shapes beyond the windshield. She leaned forward and saw a wash of stars overhead. Then the dimmed light brightened, the clearing opened up, and a whole night landscape blossomed into view.

"We're letting you go," Alden said and carried Boris's crate into the middle of the clearing. He left it there and retreated. They waited inside the camper until, finally, Boris climbed out, sniffed the air, waddled and tottered around, going first this way, then that, as if he couldn't decide. Then, all at once, he was gone.

And so were they.

It must have been the middle of the night when they got to Apple Pie Hill. Alden said that from the top of the fire tower you could see Camden and Trenton. Beyond the horizon were Philadelphia, Wilmington, and New York. Alden parked just beneath the tower. He popped Duchamp's top, folded the table up and Maisie's bed out, and crawled into his sleeping area in the back. Without Boris and the crate there was more than the usual amount of space. Maisie got into her sleeping bag. The louvered windows were open, and the night air was fresh.

When Alden began to snore Maisie slid out of her sleeping bag and went outside. She climbed the steps of the fire tower. A vast blackness spread out in all directions. Sprinkled in the distance were strings of light decorating the horizon like a beaded fringe. From the Big Dipper, she found Polaris, the North Star. A slight breeze was blowing. She could hear it in the trees. The air smelled very fresh. She understood why Alden had come here. It was peaceful. But it also felt more precarious than the turnpike, where she could reckon where she was to the nearest tenth of a mile. The forest spread out below as far and wide as the eye could see. She could see herself in the distance, soaring, overtaking the woman she would become in the decades ahead. It was no more a trick than flying was a trick. Why shouldn't a girl who can fly not also be able to see herself grown? The future was just another vantage point, like seeing the earth from above. Why shouldn't it be part of the world-about-her? Even dimly? The woman she would become would find the past as difficult to look back on as it was natural for Maisie to see her older self—if not clearly and down to the last detail, then at least as well as memory finds the past. To remember ahead felt perfectly normal. After all, aren't both future and past equally unreadable? In the end, you only make of them what you can.

THE SERVICE AREA was easy to spot from the air. It bulged out from the parallel lanes of the turnpike like something passing though the body of a snake. Alden was parked at the farthest end. Maisie found him sitting on a bench drinking coffee from a thermos. The job that had been promised him the night before had fallen through, and without Boris to feed and take care of there wasn't much to do but watch the cars and trucks and listen to the whoosh of traffic on the highway. It was astonishing how long Alden could sit and watch the world go by. Maisie used to think there was something wrong with him. He drank the last sip of coffee, twisted the cap back onto the thermos. "Well, I guess it's time to move on." He stood up, hands in his pockets, looking at some point in the distance. Maisie didn't know what to say. It made her a little sad to think that maybe he just didn't know what to do with her. "Come on," he said and started walking away.

She followed him to the side entrance of the main building. She waited for him as people hurried in and out of the restrooms. They returned to Duchamp, and Maisie lay down in the back and looked out the rear window as Alden backed up. It felt safe out on the highway, just the right combination of coming and going. Maisie asked again where they were going, and Alden said, "To Sally's house."

"Who's Sally?"

"My sister," he said.

This came as a shock. Alden had a sister?

"She's not really my sister. Sally's mom was married to my mother's brother, Jack. We grew up together. I think you're going to like her."

"Oh" was all Maisie could say. She didn't know if it made her happy or sad to learn so much all at once and so casually. Why hadn't he mentioned Sally before? And why didn't he just say they were cousins instead of putting it in a way that seemed simple but really made things a lot harder to figure out? If he'd just said they were cousins, Maisie would have understood right away. But calling her a sister and then taking it back and bringing mothers and uncles into it was a way of giving her an answer before she could figure out what was important. She was beginning to see that that was his way of putting things, hiding what was difficult behind a mask of simplicity. Maybe it came from having grown up wild. After all, nature is full of trickeries. Even the simplest birdcall or pattern of lichen growing on a rock is significant beyond what the ear can hear and the eye can see. Is it for protection that the inner workings of things are hidden? Or is it just ignorance that creates the appearance of hiddenness and makes the world seem complicated when, really, it's all very simple?

She watched the roadway unfurl behind them from Duchamp's rear window. Questions began swarming in her head—a place with cousins, aunts, and uncles. She rubbed her eyes hard and squinted through the trailing sparks and tried to stay awake. She wondered what her mother would have said about all that was happening. Would she want her to stay with Alden? Or go back to Opa and Yva? It was hard to know. With everything pressing in so vividly, it was hard to know anything. She lay down in the rear and felt black electricity tingling in all the different parts of her body. The current ran from the back of her head through her arms and down her legs to her feet. With palms pressed flat on the cushion, she could feel herself melting into the reverberating shell of the moving camper. The headlights of the cars cast moving shadows as they gained and then zoomed past in the next lane. It felt cozy to be so close to and yet feel so far removed from the hardness and speed of the road outside. The cozier she became, the less she heard of the cars whooshing past and the more she could hear of the thin cochlear siren in her own ears. She tried to keep her eyes open and stay awake. Globules of darkness drifted across her vision. Everything was tingling and floating in-side her like a dream.

Then everything was slack and loose again. Alden was lifting her up from the cushion, out of the camper, into the air. She kept her eyes closed and let her arms and legs dangle as he carried then put her down in a soft bed and covered her with a blanket under which she snuggled and curled to sleep.

It was morning when she woke up. Gauzy grey light fil-tered through a window hung with thin lace curtains. She lay there, warm under the blanket, surveying the cracked ceiling directly above the bed. A brown stain spread across it like a giant island, dark at the edges, shaded and lined with topographic details—mountains, rivers, towns, and cities. She drifted back to sleep. When she opened her eyes again the room was bright with morning sun, and a wom-an was talking in the next room.

A door opened and shut. Or a cupboard? Chair legs scooted on a wooden floor. A cough. "Damn it, Fish! Go lie down!" Dog nails clicked across the floor, a clatter of dishes. Alden's voice was muffled, as if he were chewing or propping his chin in his hand. The other voice was smoky, clear and direct. Maybe even a little happy. "Go on, Fish!"

Then silence. Maisie rubbed her eyes and stayed under the covers. The voices in the next room were suddenly lower. She couldn't make out what was being said. Were they whispering? Talking about her? She didn't care. It was cozy underneath the blanket. The talking in the next room made it even cozier. She would stay in bed for so long they would begin to worry and come tiptoeing in to check on her. They'd exchange glances, then tiptoe back out. She'd make them wait and wonder for a little while longer, then get up. They'd be so glad to see her they'd give her anything she wanted.

There was a shuffling of chairs and clattering of dishes as if a table were being set or cleared. Footsteps caused the floorboards to bounce ever so slightly. That felt cozy, too. It was cozy to be in a house that was shaky and old. A faucet was turned on, and water ran for several seconds, then cut off with a rattle of pipes. A door opened, then closed, and it went quiet. Maisie's heart began beating faster. Who was in the next room? She sat up in bed and listened. Was that Alden whistling outside? She slid out from under the covers and tiptoed over to the window. The floor was smooth, not splintery, and she felt little crumbs of dirt underfoot. Curtains of yellowed lace hung on the window. She parted them and peeked out, breathed on the fogged glass, then rubbed it with her palm. A blur of sky and trees. She held her breath and waited, waited for the sound of the van starting up. Would Alden drive away and leave her? Was he coming back? Was Sally nice? How many more things were going to happen to her? She tried to lift the window, but it was stuck. She pushed as hard as she could, not caring if the glass broke, but it wouldn't budge.

"Well, good morning." Maisie spun around and, trembling suddenly, began to cry. Everything happened quickly and in slow motion at the same time. She stiffened but didn't resist as she was gathered in arms that were soft and strong. Everything was itself and its opposite for she didn't know how long afterward. She may have closed her eyes or rubbed them so hard the tears were forced back. Everything turned black. She couldn't see and didn't want to look and was both scared and comforted. Sally held Maisie close and rocked her and said, "It's okay. It's all right," cupping the back of Maisie's head and stroking her hair.

Finally she let go and got to her feet with one of those little grunts adults give. She was wearing bell-bottoms that fit a little tightly around her thighs and a blouse with an embroidered front. Maisie drew a damp forearm across her nose, looking Sally up and down for the first time. Was she a hippie? She was pretty. Maisie wanted to run back into her arms for another long hug. But Sally touched Maisie's shoulder and said, "C'mon. I'll show you my chickens."

Passing through the house, Maisie was glad it wasn't at all what she'd imagined. It was bright, and there were lots of potted plants and old comfy furniture and pictures on the walls, lots of pictures. There was an old woodstove and a crate of split wood and newspapers scattered on the hearth and a small kitchen with a window over the sink. The first thing she noticed when she got outside was that Duchamp was still there. Alden got out and closed the side door.

"Be right back," he said and started walking up the sandy dirt drive in the leggy way he walked when he had something important to do.

"Where's he going?" Maisie asked.

"Over to his place."

"He has a place?"

Sally laughed. Maisie wanted to run and catch up, but Sally said, "C'mon," and started walking around to the back of the house. Maisie was surprised to see how big the yard was. It wasn't a lawn with grass but an open clearing that stood between the house and the scrubby pine and oak trees surrounding it on all sides. In the far corner was a wooden coop attached to the biggest cage Maisie had ever seen, a tumbled blanket of wire wrapped around and over the tops of poles stuck in the ground at all angles. It was the kind of place Maisie could imagine making all by herself, and she was a little surprised that someone as pretty as Sally would have such an ugly, falling-down-looking thing right behind her house. Sally unhooked a section of wire and peeled it back for Maisie to go through.

"There's all kinds of critters just waitin' to get in here."

"What kinds of critters?"

"You name it. Foxes. Raccoons. Snakes."

"We had a raccoon. Boris. He was probably hit by a car. Alden found him."

"What did you do with him?"

"Let him go."

She showed Maisie how to reach under the straw to feel for eggs. The hens flapped and clucked. "Feel anything?" Maisie shook her head and stepped back to let Sally try. She felt all around and then checked in the corners. "No eggs today, I guess." Sally shooed the hens away.

"It's a big cage," Maisie said, looking at the tangle.

"My hens have it good." Sally put her hands on her hips. "You like chicken?"

Maisie glanced at the hens scratching in the dirt.

"Wait'll you have one of mine. You'll know what a real chicken is."

Maisie's eyes widened.

Sally laughed. "Not them! I get my eating chickens from a friend nearby. Best you ever had." Maisie watched as she inspected, twisted and bent sections of the wire cage back into shape. The sun was coming up over the tops of the trees, and the air was suddenly alive with clouds of flying bugs. Lit up in morning light, the house did not look run-down anymore and the chicken coop wasn't a tumbled-up mess. Everything seemed tucked in and set in place right where it belonged, even the ground itself, which was a fine white sand strewn with pine needles and tufts and clumps of grass. She dug her toes into it with the grand easiness of suddenly not feeling a stranger. When she looked up Sally was going back to the house. "Come inside when you're hungry," she called.

Maisie made a circuit of the yard, planting her feet care-fully, watching where she stepped. She wondered if her mother had ever been here. There was a stunted oak tree at the far corner of the yard, gnarled and knotted and dilap-idated and lonely. The leaves were light green and tender. Two squirrels were chasing each other, leaping, grabbing, and swinging through the upper branches. They were red, not grey like the ones in Riverside Park. Alden said in the olden days Pineys used to skewer them on sticks and eat them. She wondered if that was really true.

Suddenly she heard Duchamp's door open. When it slammed shut she raced back around to the front yard yell-ing, "Wait! Wait!," rounding the corner of the house just as Alden started the engine. He leaned over and opened the passenger door for her.

"Don't panic." He smiled. "I'm not going anywhere."

Maisie was out of breath and couldn't speak. She got in with a look that said, "But here you are with the engine running."

"Get any breakfast?" Alden asked.

Maisie turned away. At the top of the drive they came to a deeply rutted track. Alden turned onto it, stopped, and began reversing up the road. He stuck his head out of the open window and drove backward, one arm hanging out. Then he ducked in, cut the wheel sharply, bounced over the ruts straight into a space between the trees, and parked in front of a large unpainted shack with shuttered windows and two cinder blocks for steps. There was a thick padlock on the door, which Alden opened with a key he dug out of his pocket.

"Come in and have a look," he said.

Curious but also a little afraid because she was barefoot, she got out. The ground was soft and damp as she tiptoed, trying not to think of snakes and spiders. The cinder blocks wobbled slightly when she stepped up to the door. It was dark and much larger than it looked from the outside. The far wall was a large sliding glass door that had been boarded up with plywood. The walls were lined with shelves made out of raw lumber, old wooden crates and boxes. In the center of the room was a large table piled with wooden panels and boxes and rolls of fabric and assorted jars and cans. There was a door on the left and above it a loft piled with things and an old wooden ladder in the corner. The place smelled strongly of what Alden later said were turps and varnishes.

He stepped into the light, holding up a painting for Maisie to see. It wasn't very big, and it swirled with all sorts of color and blotted shapes and images that looked familiar without being anything in particular. A face? It reminded Maisie of a painting in Opa and Yva's apartment. Alden took another step toward the light, and now she could see that the surface was thickly coated with swirls and gobs and things pressed into the paint. Every time he shifted and the light hit it at a different angle the image seemed to change, like something you'd see in the clouds.

"Did you paint it?" Maisie asked.

He nodded.

"What is it?"

"Your mother," he said, looking at the painting as if trying to decide something.

Maisie stared hard at the picture, waiting for it to snap into focus with the image she carried in her head, an image from photographs, especially the framed one in Opa and Yva's bedroom that showed her mother, whose name was Katherine, sitting on a rock in Central Park.

"It doesn't look like her," Maisie said.

"It doesn't have to." Alden smiled.

Maisie narrowed her eyes and tried to melt everything that was floating in her mind together. She hadn't meant to hurt his feelings. Alden started moving things around. "I guess it kind of looks like her," Maisie offered as Alden went up the ladder. He moved like someone who knew just what he wanted and exactly where it was. The paintings were stacked in wooden racks. "Recognize this?" He held up another picture that reminded her of highway signs and asphalt and patches of fox-colored rust. Alden smiled and set the painting next to the first one. Maisie didn't want to say the wrong thing again. Her eyes darted from picture to picture, trying to tease different possibilities out of the images and shapes and colors confronting her. Finally she looked up, not knowing what she saw and grateful to Alden for not asking. He put the paintings away without saying anything further. There was a certain order to the way they were kept. The more she glanced about, the more she began to see that years and years of order were stored here and that Alden seemed happy.

"Do you have any more pictures of my mother?"

"Yes. But you might not recognize her."

"Did you think she was pretty?"

Alden set the ladder in the corner. "Your mother was the

most beautiful woman I've ever known," he said. Maisie thought he was going to hug her, but he just put his hand on her shoulder and squeezed gently. After that he seemed to move more slowly, as if he were tired. Maisie wondered if she'd made him sad. Maybe she should apologize. But she didn't know what to say.

"Let's walk back," he said. They left Duchamp where he was parked, and Alden led the way down a narrow footpath in the direction of Sally's. "A shortcut," he said, then he stopped suddenly, put a finger to his lips, and pointed up into the trees.

"What is it?" Maisie whispered.

"Turkey buzzard."

The enormous bird was perched in the tree, holding its wings the way people hold their arms after an unexpected dousing; small red head, yellow-white beak like a harlequin mask, feathers gleaming black. It pretended not to see them, as if caught at an embarrassing moment. "They can sit like that for hours," Alden said, and they hurried together past the silent bird.

Sally had set Maisie's breakfast out on the table. Scrambled eggs and toast with jelly and a glass of milk. Maisie was hungry. She ate quickly while Sally sat across the table from her, smoking a cigarette and talking to Alden, who was sitting on the sofa looking through the telephone book.

She smoked Tareytons, and there were half-empty packs of them scattered all over the house.

"We can all go over there together." Sally poured Maisie some more milk. "Alden?"

He was studying the book in his lap and didn't answer.

"Damn it, Alden! Will you put that away and answer me?" She crushed her cigarette in the ashtray and stood up.

"Let's talk about it another time," he said, putting the telephone book aside.

"There isn't a whole lot of time, Alden."

"All the more reason."

"The more reason for what?"

"To think a little longer."

Sally began clearing the table. Maisie finished her milk and brought the glass over to the sink, where Sally had begun washing the dishes. The backs of her arms were a smooth, mottled pink. Alden stood up and said, "I have a few errands to run."

"Where you off to?"

"Philly."

"Philly! What for?"

"Supplies," Alden said. He signaled for Maisie to get her shoes on, stirring a hop-to-it into the air with his finger.

Maisie was glad to leave the room. Her shoes and socks were under the bed, and she crawled after them, pushing them further underneath and pressing herself against the floor, feeling the boards against her cheek. She waited to see if Alden and Sally would start arguing. When they didn't she slid back out and sat on the bed with a springy squeak. She brushed the dirt from her feet and put her socks and then her shoes on, tying and retying the laces slowly and carefully, bundling the strands into knots and bows, then slowly pulling, tugging gently on the loosening string, anticipating the satisfying bump when the knot broke and she had nothing more to wait for. Was she being wafted? Or flying? It was something like the picture of a man riding a horse that Alden had clipped to the sun visor in the camper that showed how everything can be cut up and sandwiched between a before and an after but also melted together into smooth motion. She couldn't decide which was nicer to look at, the horse and man frozen just perfectly so or thundering by and disappearing into the distance. You can't have both at the same time. You can stop time in your head and keep moving or stop moving and let time run on without you.

But often it was hard to know the difference.

THEY WALKED INTO the forest. The trees were dense, and the sun cast a lean, golden light. The ground was damp. Alden gave her a pack to carry that contained their

lunch. He carried the wooden case containing the Keuffel & Esser plane table alidade they'd bought in Philly.
The man who sold it said it had been used on Guadalca-
nal in World War II. Slung on Alden's back was a newly
stretched blank canvas. From behind he looked like something being blown through the trees. The image would stay
with Maisie, especially the light, how it pierced through the
canopy in long rods and reflected in the wavy hairgrass in
the clearing where once houses and streets and gardens had
been. She watched as he unpacked and set up his things,
fascinated by the Keuffel & Esser, which looked so scientif-
ic and part of some mysterious process. She was surprised
by how much time he spent looking through it, scribbling
notes and jotting on his maps all covered with diagrams
and drawings. They were facing the ruins of a half-buried
brick arch overgrown with vines and sedges. Alden said it
had been a mill for grinding grain. A little farther down
the stream had been a sawmill and the much larger ruins of
a paper mill. "Mills everywhere," he said.

Maisie traipsed around the area while he worked and
came across foundations and cellar holes and pipelines and
tried to imagine the vanished town and the people who once
lived there. The grass was tall and blown in light whorls of
green. Scattered everywhere were trees with trunks split
down to the base—huge, gnarled limbs growing horizon-

tally, so close to the ground they looked like they might start crawling away. She followed a trail over to the lake, stood at the edge in the soft mud. There were turtles and frogs and all sorts of animal tracks leading this way and that. And bugs, too.

She went back and settled down to watch Alden. He was still making measurements and sketching and drawing plans and diagrams, and she didn't understand anything. He worked slowly and precisely and took long looks through the little telescope set in the middle of the table and wrote down notes and lots of numbers, and Maisie figured that whatever it was he was doing was very serious. After a while he turned to her and asked if she was bored.

She shook her head.

He wiped his hands on a rag in his back pocket. "You're going to stay with Sally while I'm away," he said. "She goes back to work tomorrow, so you'll be alone during the day."

"You're leaving?"

"Just for a few days."

Maisie watched a bug that was climbing a stalk of grass. There was a rusty Coca-Cola bottle cap in the grass next to her. She plucked it out and brushed it off. "I miss Opa and Yva," she said. It came out just like that. She hadn't been thinking it. But there it was.

Alden sat down next to her. "Want me to take you back?"

Maisie didn't know. She rubbed the bottle cap on her pants until it was completely smooth. She handed it to Alden, who examined it for a moment, then put it in his pocket. "I promised to take you back right away if you asked," he said.

Maisie wasn't sure anymore how long she'd been gone— if it had been weeks or months or only just days. It was true. Alden had promised. Yva kept saying they were crazy to let her go and told Alden he'd need a court order if he wanted to keep her. Then she changed her mind and said maybe it would be all right. Opa thought it was a fine idea from the start. "But only as long as everybody's happy." They'd been talking back and forth to Alden on the telephone for days. Finally he just came over and asked Maisie if she'd like to spend the summer with him. Opa said Alden had a right. Yva pressed her lips together and said, "Having a right doesn't make it right." Opa asked Maisie if she'd like to spend some time with Alden. "There are good reasons for you to get to know him and for him to get to know you." Maisie had seen Alden only a few times before and had a hard time thinking of him as her father. But she liked him. He was calm and spoke gently and seemed like someone who had been alone for a long time. Not lonely, just by himself. Mostly she liked him because she knew that if her mother were alive they would all be together again, and going with Alden was a way to sort of make that happen.

They sat in the grass. "Are you nearly finished?" Maisie asked.

"Not even started." Alden rested his chin on his knees like someone contemplating a leap into the water. Then he stood up and dusted himself off and went back to work.

Thoughts flashed in Maisie's mind of saying good-bye to Alden and Sally and going back home. Watching him work was not her idea of fun at all. Flying was. At the rest stops it had been easy to slip away when it was dark and Alden was at work. At the rest stops she had been invisible, even with people and cars all around and trucks whizzing past. She liked being out there, open to the stars, those tiny points that drew her up and up and up. She also missed her friends and the playground in Riverside Park and flying under the George Washington Bridge, skimming low along the river, passing boats and dodging gulls and geese, then zooming up up up like a rocket until she could see down the entire length of Manhattan, suspended in the air like one of those stained-glass angels in the cathedral of Saint John the Divine.

"Let's look around," Alden said, and he gave Maisie a little tour.

Beyond the ruined grist mill was a large cellar hole surrounded by trees. "One of the Harris brothers lived in a mansion here. The other one lived in his own mansion just over there." Alden pointed through the trees. "The workers' houses were down that way. More than a hundred people lived here." They stood at the rim of a shallow depression. Maisie tried to imagine a busy town there but couldn't.

"What happened to it all?"

"It all burned down in 1914. The mill was already abandoned, and nobody lived here except a man named Mahlon Broome. He lived here all alone with his wife. Before it burned down it was a YMCA summer camp. Old Broome used to bring the boys up here in his horse cart."

"How do you know?"

"My father was one of them. Your other grandfather." He smiled.

Maisie was surprised. It had never occurred to her that she had another grandfather. "Think he stood right here where we are?"

"Sure, he did. But everything looked very different then."

"What happened to your father?" Maisie asked.

"My parents died in a car accident down near Lower Bank when I was thirteen. That's why I went to live with Uncle Jack at Sally's."

They looked at each other, and everything seemed halted. It wasn't clear if it was something Alden had been wanting to say or something that had just come out. He didn't seem sad or regretful. Maisie could see that he would have told her anything she wanted to know right then and there, but she couldn't think of anything to ask, and she wondered if that hurt his feelings.

He went back to work for a little while longer and then announced it was time go. A man and a woman with binoculars passed by. "Birders," Alden said. He gave Maisie a glass jar and showed her how to clean the brushes he'd used and wrap them in cloth to keep them soft. He packed the equipment up in the wooden crate, rolled up the maps and the canvas, and led them back to Duchamp.

On the way home they stopped at a little store named Buzby's. A group of old men were sitting around on the front porch talking. "That your little girl?" one of the men asked. Alden put his hand on Maisie's shoulder and introduced her to the group. They smiled and nodded the way old men smile and nod when they don't have anything else to say. As they were about to go inside the store one of the men asked, "You following this Jetport thing, Alden?"

"A little," Alden said, holding the door for Maisie to go inside.

"They want to build the damn thing right here. Send

in fast trains to get people here from New York and all the way down to Richmond."

The other man said, "Them supersonics'll hold five hundred people and fly over to Europe in three hours."

"Never happen," one of the men said under his breath. He was carving a block of wood in his lap.

"What makes you so sure, Ed?"

"Won't happen if I have anything to do with it."

"You going to get out there with your duck gun and hold 'em off?"

"Why the hell not?"

The men all laughed.

"Damn runway's going right through your house, Ed."

"All our houses."

"I worked on jets when I was in the navy," said the man carving the wood. "In Korea."

"Guess that makes you an expert."

"Ed's expert in most things."

"They can't fly them things supersonic over land. That's why they want it here, close to the water, so they can go supersonic."

"They say they can have it built under ten years. By '76."

"Never happen."

"Why not, Ed?"

"Well, 'cause we don't have the planes, for one! Haven't

built one goddamn plane yet. The French and the Russkies have 'em. But over here it ain't nothing but drawings and a lot of goddamn noise. Charley'll have that garvey he's been workin' on forever built before even one of them things gets made!"

"Charlie's garvey!"

The men laughed again.

Inside, Alden talked to an old lady with swollen ankles. Her name was Paula. She gave Maisie a piece of honey-comb, and Alden bought two Cokes that they took back to Duchamp to drink. They sat at the table with the doors open. The men sitting on the porch across the street could see right inside. One of them waved, and Maisie waved back. She asked Alden where he was going away to, and he said he had some work to do and would be back in a few days.

"Can I come?"

"Would you want that?"

"Maybe."

They finished their Cokes, and Alden took the empty bottles back into Buzby's. On the way out he stopped and talked to the men on the porch again, but Maisie couldn't hear what they were saying. They drove back to Sally's on a dirt road that narrowed and narrowed and was like being in a tunnel. Maisie put her hand out the window to touch the tree branches as they brushed against Duchamp's side mirror. Even though the forest was shady, it was hot and everything had that flat, washed-out midday look

MAISIE LIKED HER room at Sally's. She liked lying on the bed with the sagging mattress and the springs squeaking underneath her. She liked the musty quilt. She didn't mind being all alone in the house, either, or in bed, looking up at the stain on the ceiling. She didn't mind being alone with nobody around but Fish, who slept most of the day, and the chickens clucking and pecking outside in the dirt. There was food in the fridge and an old RCA television to watch and books to read and woods to explore.

The pine barrens were perfect for daytime flying, not only because they were flat and went for miles and miles in every direction and the sky was wide open and clear but because she could fly as low as she liked without having to worry about being seen from the ground. Shortly after Sally left for work the first day, Maisie ran outside, leapt, and circled the house a few times, calling "Hey, Fishie Fishie Fishie" to the bewildered animal, who sat in the middle of the yard, following with the rapt attention dogs save for sticks and balls and tempting morsels of food. Maisie soon found herself over wild bogs and swamps and pygmy pines so low to the ground she could zoom over them at under twenty feet. She felt like Gulliver flying over those dwarf trees. It wasn't just the trees that were small but the undergrowth as well. Even the sand was tiny, as powdery as confectioner's sugar, and it sprouted tiny plants with odd shapes and textures, leaves that were like pins, and scaly bark that looked like snakeskin. In places the air had a charred smell. There were signs of fire wherever the trees were sparse. There were blueberries and blackberries and dewberries and bog after bog of cranberries. Maisie avoided the farms but skimmed low over the wild and abandoned bogs, darting this way and that like a swallow.

But it was hard keeping track of her location over the vast stretches of pine forest and swampland. There were rivers and creeks and foot trails and dirt roads. Finding her way meant staying high enough to see the broader landscape but low enough to see features on the ground—narrow gashes in the forest that were the remnants of old trails and stagecoach routes and big gashes that were paved, numbered roadways. Then there was all that wasn't there anymore—all the ruins being taken over by forest.

Sally brought a chicken home from work that day. Maisie came into the kitchen and watched her prepare it.

"How was it today? Everything go all right?"

Maisie said yes and patted Fish, who had come out from behind the sofa and was waiting to be fed.

"Did you get outside today at all?"

"A little."

"We'll do a tick check soon as I'm finished. When I was your age I spent all day in the woods."

They went into the bathroom, and Maisie stripped, and Sally checked under her arms and behind her neck and legs. No ticks, she said, then filled the tub and put in some Mr. Bubble and whipped it up into a big froth. Maisie sank into the water up to her chin and made herself a bubble beard and a bubble hat and stayed in the bath until her fingers and toes were all crinkled and Sally called her to dinner.

They ate at the kitchen table. "Do you have any children?" Maisie asked.

Sally looked a little surprised, then shook her head. "I used to think I would someday, but I kinda like being free."

They cleared the table. Sally put on the radio and sang while they washed the dishes. When they finished cleaning up, they watched Batman and Bewitched on television. A little while later, as Maisie was getting ready for bed, Alden called. Sally handed her the phone.

"Are you on the turnpike?" Maisie asked him.

"No. I'm up in Passaic."

"What are you doing?"

"I'm touring the monuments. Everything okay?"

"When are you coming back?"

"Probably not until sometime next week."

"Have you seen any raccoons?"

"No. Just cats. They're all over the place. Are you still feeling homesick?"

"No."

"When I get back we're going on an adventure together."

"What kind of adventure?"

"You'll see. It's a surprise."

The next day it rained. There was nothing for Maisie to do but stay in bed. She looked at Sally's magazines and read a book and watched some TV and played with Fish and went out to the henhouse to look for eggs. She explored the house, went upstairs into Sally's bedroom. The closet had lots of boxes, but she was afraid Sally would know if she took them out and opened them. The dresser was made of dark wood with tarnished brass handles and looked like something handed down. Maisie opened the drawers slowly, from bottom to top. There wasn't anything in the lower dresser drawers except clothes and underwear. In the middle drawer she found some jewelry hidden in an old sock. The top drawers were too high for her to see into. She dragged over the chair that Sally used to hang her clothes on and stood on it. A gun. Shiny black, the kind that cowboys used, with a cylinder and a long barrel. She touched a finger to it, was tempted to pick it up but too afraid. It was cold and smooth and scary. Maisie had never seen or touched anything like it. On TV the police always picked up guns they found with handkerchiefs and held them between two fingers like something disgusting. Why did Sally have a gun? Had she ever used it? Did she need it? Was she a criminal? Maisie stared for a while longer, then slowly closed the drawer. On top of the dresser were pictures of Sally as a little girl with her parents. There was also one of Alden and Sally as teenagers with a motorboat in the background. Alden looked pale and skinny. Sally looked skinny, too. They looked like brother and sister, squinting at the camera.

She climbed down and put the chair back. The gun and the pictures left her with a funny feeling. She went outside and sat on the front porch. It began drizzling; then it poured, then drizzled again. She tried to imagine all the many ways there were of being bored. At home she had the whole city right outside her window, humming and buzzing. Even with nothing to do, there was always knowing that things were going on everywhere all around.

After a while it stopped raining. The sun broke through the clouds, and the yard began to steam. Maisie walked barefoot out into the yard. The sand was soft and silky, and she stepped on thick tufts of grass, feeling the support in the arches of her feet. Long rays of sunlight shone straight down, bringing out different shades of green in the dripping foliage. She took the air in deep breaths and felt herself rise slowly from the ground. She began to spiral on a thermal current that bore her upward until the house was just a small feature in an ocean of green that extended to the horizon in every direction. She felt a pulsing in her arms, which she held out like wings. There were no flaps or ailerons or lift or roll spoilers, no struts or bracing wires or blades or rotors or downy feathers or silky sails. Just the simple, primal sensation of moving air and dissolving bonds, a sharpness and clarity of vision, a harmonizing resonance with things passing overhead and underneath. The ground fell away. She was part of an interflowing tapestry made up of shapes, sensations, and textures, all present and simultaneous, vivid and vague.

Alden's shack looked bigger from the air. Tucked behind old pitch pines with a magnolia tree on one side that looked as if it were growing straight out of the foundation, it backed onto the remnant of an old cranberry bog. The shack had a rusted tin roof and was sided with blackened cedar boards that Sally said had never seen a drop of paint. She said a family had lived there a long time ago and that the house was built from cedars taken from the swamp when it was turned into a cranberry farm. "In 1883, by a man named Hazelton Birdsall," she said. "He was famous for the houses he built all over these parts. Had a sideline building coffins, too. My dad used to say there was as much of Haze Birdsall's work underground as on top of it. And some that went off to sea, too, in ships built over to Lower Bank. He built the Bulltown glass factory and sawmill and houses for the people who worked in them."

"Did he build your house, too?" Maisie asked.

Sally shook her head. "That house came later. My dad bought it and the land around it just a few years before I was born. The Birdsall place wasn't even listed on the deed, which is just the way we've always kept it. A secret."

Maisie liked the enclosed, grown-in feeling of the shack, and she wondered what Alden would say if he found her there. What harm could there be in making it her own little hideaway? She had a tin of saltine crackers, a thermos with cranberry juice. Sitting on the rear stoop, she was no more visible than a frog or a turtle or any other wild creature inhabiting the boggy silence.

The woods were silent and littered with secrets—the ruins of houses, mills, factories, and towns. It was something to see a chimney sticking up out of the ground or come across a cellar hole filled with water or see a tumbled pile of rotting boards that was a house that had, in Sally's words, "grown down." It was something else to know what had once been there and to wonder what these grown-down places held in the way of forgotten memories.

SALLY WENT OFF to work every morning and made supper every night when she came home. They always ate together. Maisie began to think that Sally was not an aunt but more of a mom or a big sister. One evening they drove down to Egg Harbor City in Sally's Willys and had ice cream at a place called Al's. As they were licking their cones out front Sally asked if Maisie had noticed that the roads were all named after cities in Germany.

"Why?"

Sally shrugged as if to say the rest was self-explanatory. Like Alden, she had a way of telling you what she thought without speaking. If it was funny or obvious she grinned and her eyes sparkled and she looked for the same sparkle in Maisie. If it was something ordinary or unimportant she'd give a little shrug and move on. She had a little roll in her belly and drove holding the steering wheel with both hands, not nervous but alert. Even when she was smoking she'd keep both hands on the wheel, taking her smoldering Tareyton for a quick puff, then gently pressing it back between the stubby metal rills of the tip-out ashtray in the dashboard. Her toenails were painted bright red. Maisie wondered if her mother had been anything like Sally and hoped they were somehow alike.

The evening air was thick with mosquitoes, and the windshield was spattered with bugs. "All the old families here go way back," Sally said as they passed through Week-stown. "Cavileers, Sooys, Leeks, and Weeks." She drove very slowly over an old iron bridge and turned onto River Road. "The Green Bank Hotel, the Hester Anne Ford and Updike houses are all gone," she said. "But the Sooy Hol-laway place and the Wobbar store and the Sooy Crowley place are still here." She pointed to one of the old houses. "My friend Betty used to live there. She was five years old-er, but we were friends anyway. She went to Hollywood, and you can see her in all the big TV shows. Bonanza. The Virginian. I have a picture of her at home. I'll show it to you. She signed it personally to me. The Wobbars are re-lated to the Birdsalls are related to the Crowleys are related to the Sooys all the way back." Maisie looked at the house. It had a steep, gabled roof and lots of windows and a big front porch. "Imagine seeing sailing ships on the river," Sally said. "They used to build them right here. Tall wood-en ships with sails."

They drove on. There was nothing to look at but cat-tails and a bend in the river. "There were all sorts of big plans for this place," Sally said. "Used to be a busy harbor. Ships took stuff to Philadelphia, New York. Lumber, iron, paper and glass, fish, and oysters. Big ships with masts and sails; steamships, too. They were going to build a whole city here with streets and avenues, parks and schools. A big glass factory got built but went right out of business the same year it opened, 1879. The railroad that was supposed to pass through here never got built. A couple of houses were still here when I was a kid. Now it's nothing left." She went quiet for a minute. Then she took her hand from the wheel and touched Maisie's shoulder and said, "That's what makes it special, honey. Not built over like other places. Just gone."

She took Maisie out to other places that weren't there anymore, places with names that sounded like they weren't meant to be known to anyone except the people who had lived and died there. Ong's Hat, Tabernacle, Atsion, and Batsto, which was being fixed up and turned into a kind of museum. "My dad wanted me and Alden to leave like everybody else. But the fact there's nothing left doesn't depress me at all. In a funny way, that's what makes it more real. The fact that it's gone. What's important is what stays in here." Sally tapped her forehead. "With memories you always have a place to spend the night in."

Maisie didn't understand what Sally meant. But that

didn't matter. It was a lot like flying. If you thought too much, getting off the ground was impossible. They drove back through Green Bank and Wading River and Leektown, where Sally drove straight into the forest as if it were the most normal thing in the world to do.

"Where are we going?" Maisie asked.

"One of the most forgotten places around here." Sally kept her eyes fixed on the track ahead. She drove without talking, steering around holes and ditches and dodging fallen branches. It seemed to Maisie that Sally was concentrating both on the track in front of them and on something private very far away. After they'd gone a good distance Sally began pointing out details of the forest, beginning with the twenty different kinds of huckleberries that grew everywhere and how different they all tasted. In another month, Sally said, they'd be able to drive through and pick berries without even getting out of the jeep. Just pick them right through the window. She pointed through the trees to a clearing in the distance. "That's all savannah bottom over there. Solid clay. No trees'll grow in it. Just grass and grouseberries, which it'll be full of now. And ducks. They live in the swamps but breed in the upland." As she was about to drive on a flock of ducks suddenly rose up into the air, and Sally turned to Maisie with a just-so look, and they laughed together at the perfect timing of it all.

They stopped where some wooden logs had been laid across the road. She pointed into the woods around them. "These are turkey oaks. They only grow where the water is just below the surface. Low wet bottom. That's why these logs were laid down here." Then she got out and walked over the logs, bouncing to test them. When she'd gone a good distance she stopped and put her hands on her hips. Maisie wondered if she saw Sally walking along a city sidewalk, if she would look just as sprung right out of the earth and being just the way she liked to be. Sally came back, and they drove slowly over the logs. "See those trees up ahead? Red cedar. Grows on high ground. Won't grow in wet bottom. Means it's dry up ahead. Not many red cedars around anymore. Most were cut and cleared out of here long ago. Those ones up there. They're real old."

"How do you know so much about the forest?" Maisie asked.

"When I was your age I wanted to be a woodjin."

"What's a woodjin?"

"Someone who lives from the woods. Not in but from. Like an injin."

Maisie looked up into the canopy. The tops of the trees glowed a thick orange light that seemed brushed on. Flying gave a completely different impression of the forest. Skimming low, the trees were part of the tapestry of the ground, different textures and hues that fitted into a larger picture. Maisie hadn't thought of their individual characters and traits: the way they contain and reveal things about the ground they grow up from the way people contain and reveal the places they grow up in and, in spite of all their mobility, never really leave.

Sally pointed to some trees she said were non-native, put there by people. "Cherry, mainly." There were grapevines everywhere. She pointed them out as if it saddened her to see them. "They kill everything off. Weave through the old trees and choke them off." Then she began to name all the different kinds of pine she knew: princess pine, crawling pine, standing pine, shortleaf pine, cross pine, pitch pine. She especially liked cedars. Red because it grows so slowly and can live for hundreds of years. And white, which she called swamp cedar. "You can still smell it in the attic of my house a hundred years later."

A little farther on she stopped suddenly and turned off the engine. "Martha Furnace," she said and got out. Some trees had been cut down, and what looked like a small brick room about the height of a man was being dug out of a grown-over embankment. "It's an archaeological excavation," Sally said proudly. "I've been coming out to help. Been digging here since spring." They walked around the half-uncovered ruin and over to a cellar hole and then to a pile over in the trees that she called a "slag heap left over from the iron-making process." She pointed to the grape-killed trees that weren't native—maple, chokecherry—and to a ditch she called a sluiceway. "Five hundred people once lived and worked right here. We're trying to find a cemetery. Some think it's over in Calico. With that many people living here you'd think there'd be graves somewhere. But so far, nothing."

The sun was getting low, and the forest echoed with the hollow sounds of approaching evening. They stood by a little stream and looked at the reddish water peppered with spindle-legged bugs darting over the surface. Sally put a hand on Maisie's shoulder. Maisie felt awkward and didn't know what to do, so she put her arm around Sally, and they stood there for a few minutes in an uncertain softness. It seemed to go on forever but then ended quickly. They got back in the car, and Sally pointed out what she called sloughs and spongs, places in the forest where water collected or flowed. They went through an area that had burned recently. The charred trees looked ghoulish—twisted, gnarled stumps sticking out of the ground. The smell grew stronger and stronger, and even the ground was black and scorched. Then, suddenly, they came to a paved road, and the air smelled sweet again. Sally pointed at the unburned trees on the other side of the road. "I'd say we got out of there just in time." She smiled without looking at Maisie, who understood she was being teased but also drawn into something they would always have between them.

FROM THE AIR a man riding a bicycle looks like something a bird might eat. Rolling through the pinewoods with his maps and canvas strapped to his back, gripping the wide handlebars, Alden could have been some kind of exotic bog insect. Maisie hung back. The path curved and narrowed in places like a tunnel and widened in stretches, and the forest thinned and was more open to the sky, and Maisie felt herself being drawn up and pinned against it like a kite.

She was riding a brand-new bicycle, a red Stingray with a banana seat that Alden had brought as a present. In the morning before they'd set out, he'd shown her a map with a tiny puddle of blue stamped all around with green and brown lines.

"Is that where we're going?"

"If we can find it," he said. He was living again in his shack. Maisie had helped him move in. Together they took down the plywood from the windows, swept and aired the place out. Alden was one of those people who could make himself comfortable anyplace. He slept on an old mattress and had a wooden cranberry crate for a bedside table.

There was a lamp with a yellowed shade, a piece of carpet, and shelves made out of pine boards for his books. There were lots of books. He kept his clothes folded neatly in a cedar chest and hung his winter clothes and work overalls on pegs in the wall. There was a small stove and a sink but no bathtub or shower—just an outhouse at the back next to the magnolia tree. He was never dirty or unclean but had that unwashed look that can seem stylish on certain types of people who don't care what others think.

Maisie spent the next days shuttling back and forth from Sally's on her new bike, bringing Alden messages and things to eat. She sat for hours out on the back stoop, watching over the bog while Alden worked. He had a radio that he kept tuned to a classical music station. It sounded strange, not at all part of the scenery. She liked watching ducks land out on the watery corner of the bog, the way they came in holding their wings cupped in little arches, then dropped, webfeet forward, skied along the surface, and settled down, moving from the element of the air to the element of the water like a bridge between two worlds. Maisie felt like a bridge, too—between the Sally world in which she was a comfortable guest and the Alden world, where she only had the feeling of looking in. Then there was home, where she also felt kind of like a guest—a loved one but, still, a guest. Now she was a bridge between that city home, a world of air conditioning, elevators, hallways, and sidewalks, and this harder place laid right out in the open but also settled onto the earth, a place where you could live quietly forever.

Alden had a pocket compass and showed Maisie how to use it. He also showed her how to find south using a watch if there was no compass handy and how to read a topo map. Topo maps were important in Alden's world, especially his "seven-and-a-halfs," big sheets he marked up and drew and sketched and made all sorts of notes on. "They go with the work," he said. Maisie didn't understand and watched as he studied his maps and diagrams spread out on the ground. The pine trees were thick and rose out of dense underbrush. He pointed to a dashed line with a twig he'd picked out of the dirt. Maisie tried to recall what Sally had told her about hard and soft bottomland and grape-killed plants. But it all ran together in her head.

"Are we lost?"

"That would be fun, wouldn't it?" Alden patted her on the shoulder. "Don't worry." The sun was high, and under the shaded canopy it was growing hot and clammy. Gnats swarmed. Alden took an apple out of his bag, broke it in two with his bare hands, and gave half to Maisie. Then he drew five circles in the sand and named them: "Point. Position. Place. Region. Space."

He made five more circles below the first ones and labeled them: "Position. Place. Body. Region. Space."

"See the difference?"

"No point?"

Alden laughed. "Exactly. Instead of putting place in the middle—which is how most people look at maps—put body in the middle." He drew a line between the two rows of circles. "Body is you—blindfolded and standing in the middle of a room." They stood looking down at the circles for a few moments. "I'm pretty sure that's how animals do it," he said and tossed the stick away. She watched as he secured all the gear on his bike, noticing, not for the first time, how brand-new hers looked next to his. She felt proud that he'd given it to her, proud to have it and to be part of what he was doing.

They rode on for a while and then stopped again so that Alden could make notes. He took compass readings, sketched in lines, and pointed out where they were headed, the little blue patch that Maisie hoped would be a cool, shady pond to swim in and not a dark amber puddle. A slight breeze was blowing but not enough to cool anything. Alden was sweating. His shirt was soaked and clung to his back. The light had that summer-afternoon gauziness that made her wish she could be back at Sally's. Alden's bike was loaded down and heavy. Maisie worried that he might topple over. It was funny to think of him riding through the woods with his maps and his easel and his paints, out of place but somehow also welcome. Flying was very much like riding a bicycle through the woods, too. The sky was filled with things that didn't belong there. A helicopter was as impossible and incongruous a sight as a bat or a pelican or a hummingbird. Somehow they all get up into the air. Can't say exactly how. But somehow they do.

At last the trail ended. Alden took out his compass, pointed through the trees, and said, "Over there."

"What about the bikes?"

"We'll leave them."

Maisie sat on her bike and watched Alden unpack his gear. He wore the same expression out at the rest stops with his brooms and mops. He didn't look tired or old or broken down the way some people look doing the things nobody likes doing, but he did seem like someone who felt those things, had set them aside and discovered something worthwhile that lay beyond them. When everything was gathered up he tied a red ribbon high on a tree branch, and they set off through the woods.

Maisie followed, whacking the underbrush with a sturdy stick Alden handed her. She imitated him, stirring and parting the low-hanging branches, probing the ground with firm pokes and jabs. Her eyes were trained and focused in the middle distance. The rustle of their footsteps in the foreground; overhead the sounds of life in the canopy; and then, all of a sudden, a clearing. Tall grass and reeds and blue sky. Alden pushed straight into it. The ground became soft, and they sank into it. She stepped in his footsteps, hopping and using her stick for balance. Two ducks burst into the air just a few yards ahead and flew off. Then Maisie and Alden were standing on a mound at the edge of a rippling plate of clear water.

From the air they would have looked like some invading species of large animal. The cattails and reeds were tamped down in a circle around them. A fallen cedar formed a dam that was part of the inflow or outflow from the pond. Alden said there were probably older, bigger cedars submerged under the pond, trees that had been put there a long time ago and never excavated and dragged out. Cedar mining, he called it, but didn't explain how or why it was that trees were mined. Maisie still couldn't make sense of what he was doing—sketching and diagramming as if revising and changing the landscape itself. She looked around and began to explore. In the reeds by the water she saw a large snake curling along beside her. She raced back to Alden, who said, "Don't worry, there aren't any poisonous snakes around here anymore."

But she stayed away from the water after that. Two or

three times she asked what he was doing, not because she expected an answer but simply out of boredom. He began telling her about an old man with a large, droopy mustache, a man named Cobb who'd made his living trapping turtles. "Fykin' turkles," he said. Maisie laughed at his changed accent, a country twang she'd never heard him use before. She thought it was fake, but as he went on she realized it wasn't fake at all but more like the residue of something people from here would recognize whether they'd known old Snapper Cobb or not. Then he told her about fishing for mossbunkers. "Greentails, people called 'em. Used to run up the Mullica. We ate 'em smoked or pickled." He told her about snapping turtles as old as the Civil War and homemade wooden boats called garveys and sneakboxes and old Charley Weber, the last of the salt hayers, who lived "down to Lower Bank and tied his barge near the old shipyard down to River Road back when tall-masted schooners still sailed down from New York for things that aren't grown or made or even remembered anymore. All long gone and forgotten."

Maisie listened carefully, could see it all so well.

"And then what?" she wanted to know.

"And then nothing," he said and waved his arm at the bog and trees. "You don't have to have existence to exist. This is it."

What a disappointment. It made her feel sad. What sort of people only talked about what was gone? As if they liked it better. Didn't they like what was here? Should she stop listening? The uneasy feeling stayed with her and kept her awake that night even though she was exhausted from being outside in the heat all day. She thought about the picture Alden had made of her mother. She still didn't know what to think about it, but it was also something she couldn't stop thinking about. Even if it didn't look like her mother at all, it somehow showed her—and like everything else around the place also showed something that was gone. The next morning when he came to get her she said she didn't feel well and wanted to stay inside. He sat down on the edge of the bed and asked if she was homesick. Maisie shook her head and plucked at the sheets, unable to explain. After he and Sally had left for the day, she went outside to check the henhouse for eggs and pick some flowers. Then she went with the flowers over to Alden's place to put them in a jar and look at the painting of her mother. The windows were all shut and it was dark inside, but he'd left the door unlocked, and she knew where everything was and what to do.

THAT AFTERNOON MAISIE flew higher than she'd ever flown before, was borne upward in a column of warm air to an altitude she'd never experienced. The sky was clear and, except for long, cigar-shaped wisps, nearly cloudless. She circled the house on that fat column of warm air, taking in everything she could. She let herself rise until her ears began to throb and the pressure in her head could no longer be equalized. She'd never seen the horizon at such a distance or felt so empty and free of the world's weight. The land was green and brown and yellow, cut by roads and the snaking Mullica River, which meandered through the flat plain and emptied into the tidal estuaries and channels and inlets and became open ocean beyond Great Bay.

The corkscrewing, vertical ascent left her dizzy and with a hollow pit in her stomach. The warm air she was sitting on was comfortable, like an overstuffed cushion, but she was afraid to rise any higher on it. Her ears throbbed. She dove, twisting and twisting downward until the pressure in her head equalized and she saw Alden sitting on the fallen tree trunk, chin in hand, staring across the pond from the semicircle of tamped-down grass and muddy ground. She hovered above him for a time. Should she circle overhead and call down to him? Hey Alden! Look up here! He would gape up, then stagger to his feet. "Maisie! Maisie!" She'd dart in circles around him, just out of reach. He'd jump up, trying to touch her, carried away completely. He'd hurl all his drawings and maps skyward, send them sailing out over the pond, not caring where they landed.

Or should she drop down silently right behind him and shout BOO! Or come up very quietly and whisper in his ear—Alden—and see him fall over backward off the log. Would he be angry? Or would he laugh and ask, "Where did you come from?" And she would smile and point nowhere in particular and leave him guessing. Or what would happen if she landed in front of him? Dropped down, just like that. As if it were the most natural thing in the world to do. Plop. There'd be astonishment and surprise, but it would eventually wear off, and the whole useless question of what next would become the focus and distraction forever after. What do we do now? would become the single, stupid, all-consuming question of their whole existence and ruin everything. Even if she could get him to just accept her as she was, the question would always be lurking, waiting to be acted on. What next? What do we do now? Would he be able just to love her—and not just because she could fly?

Maisie hovered just outside the periphery of Alden's vision. Should she withdraw to a safer distance? Move gradually from the periphery to the center and let him blink and rub his eyes and disbelieve? She could keep just enough distance that he would think it was his eyes playing tricks, a mirage caused by shimmering bog air. She could dart in and out of view, disappear and reappear, skim over the surface of the pond, rise up out of the forest. He'd think he was going crazy. She smiled at the thought. Would it be mean to trick him like that? To be really mean, she'd have to fly right up in front of him. Do stunts. Loop-de-loop. Fly upside down. But that could only end badly since, after taunting him like that, when he really went crazy she'd have to drop a boulder on his head to put him out of his misery.

There was higher and lower, underneath and upside down. Then there was back home on the sofa with the attic fan turned on full. She'd drunk a pitcher-full of lemonade, gone outside twice to soak herself with the hose, and didn't care if Sally scolded her for not wiping her muddy footprints off the floor. Fish was lying on his side on the rug, chugging away like a furry bellows, stopping abruptly now and then with a slurp of his big tongue. Did dogs get out of breath from panting too hard? Sally burst through the door. When she saw Maisie and Fish sprawling under the fan she let out a "Whooee! It's hot" and plucked at her blouse. "Get your suit on, girl. We're going to the beach." Maisie sat up. Her head throbbed. Sally went upstairs and came back down a few minutes later wearing a long tee shirt over a bathing suit and flip-flops.

It was all too fast.

"Can you believe this heat?" Sally asked, and they were

off to the beach. Sally seemed all wound up and drove faster than usual, letting her cigarette burn down in the ashtray
and complaining cheerfully about her day, then talking
about a deer that used to go into the Acme in Barnegat and
eat the produce right off the rack. "A full-grown doe. Right
through the front door. Completely unafraid of people."

The Manahawkin causeway was heavy with traffic. As
they approached Ship Bottom, Sally put her head out the
window and said, "Ahhh." Maisie wondered if she was being funny. Unlike the woods, where she knew things, here
Sally just glided along with an elbow out the window. The
road ended in a parking lot. Sally said it was the best spot
because the beach was less crowded. They took the beach
bag and a blanket and walked across the hot sand toward
the water. The tide was coming in, and the sun was behind
them. The ocean sparkled. When they'd spread the blanket
and set their things down, Sally shouted, "Race ya!" and
they ran splashing into the surf, holding hands and laughing as the waves broke against their backs. An old biplane
flew overhead pulling a banner that read "Mom wants a
Magnavox." It felt to Maisie as if time had slowed. Even
the foamy fizzle of the surf felt like something happening
in slow motion, far off at a distance. It was the first time
she had ever been to the ocean. She wanted to tell Sally,
who was lying on her stomach with her chin propped on

her fist. Her skin was mottled and bluish pink, and in her bikini she looked fatter and ruddier than she did with her clothes on. Maisie wondered if when she got breasts they would flatten and press out white from her sides when she was lying down like that, and if she'd get freckles across her shoulders, and if the bottoms of her feet would be so hard and cracked. She wanted to thank Sally for bringing her, but the longer they lay there side by side, the less Maisie felt like saying anything that might make her look pathetic. Being there was all that mattered. Calling attention to it would be like calling attention to Sally's thighs.

"Look! Dolphins!" Sally sprang to her feet and pointed to a line of fins rolling lazily a short distance offshore. Maisie followed Sally down to the water's edge. "Actually, I think they're porpoises."

The line of grey triangles broke the surface of the water, then rolled back under.

"What's the difference?" Maisie asked.

"I don't know," Sally said. "Maybe there isn't any."

How could someone know so many different kinds of pine tree and not know the difference between a porpoise and a dolphin? It seemed wrong. Later, walking in the surf, Maisie wondered how someone could live so close to the ocean and not come all the time. She thought of Alden out in the hot, snaky bog. Did he ever come to the shore where there were biplanes and people and fun things to do? How much a person missed by favoring one place over another. Sally stooped to pick up a seashell, and then another, and then another. Maisie copied her, and they walked on the beach sharing their finds until it was nearly dark. Then they got back in the Willys and drove home.

They saw the red-and-blue streaks of light flashing and flickering through the trees as they came around the bend. Sally slowed down for a moment, then said, "Holy Christ!" She jammed her foot on the gas and raced down the road, gripping the wheel and saying, "No no no. Please, God, no."

The way was blocked by a police car parked just above the turn into Sally's road—far enough away for them not to see the full complement of trucks and vehicles but close enough to see that it wasn't Sally's but Alden's place that was burning. Maisie turned to Sally, squinting into the flashing police beacon. "Stay here," Sally said and got out of the car. A man emerged in that slow, deliberate way police have of getting in and out of their cars. He had a flashlight. Maisie couldn't hear what they were saying and watched the pantomime and the beam of light flashing down the road. She shrank down into her seat. Sally and the policeman were arguing. The policeman seemed more irritated than sympathetic, shaking and cocking his head. At last he held up both hands, patted the air as if assenting but promising nothing.

Sally stalked back, shaking her head. "Asshole," she muttered. She slumped behind the wheel and burst into tears. Maisie was crying, too. There was ocean salt and tear salt, and the colored lights were just a smear across the darkness.

"Did you go over there today?" Sally asked.

Maisie felt a lump in her throat and a sudden rearrangement and distraction of all her thoughts.

"Did you go there today?" Sally asked again.

Maisie realized she should have answered the first time. But she couldn't speak. She couldn't say no or yes because it wasn't no or yes that was being asked but something else, something different; and she couldn't answer Sally's question without answering other things first, things she didn't understand and maybe never would.

The door of the police car opened, and Sally got out again. The policeman didn't bother with his flashlight this time, and there was none of the earlier agitation. Sally listened and looked at the ground and nodded. Maisie tried to hear what was being said but couldn't over the thrumming fire trucks. If she flew away now they'd think she was the Jersey Devil and blame her for everything, and she'd have to fly to some remote corner of the pine barrens and hide out forever. Sally returned to the car with a furrowed look. Maisie hung her head, and her chin began to quiver. She'd never be able to explain and she felt Sally's eyes fixed on her and she couldn't look into them but she also couldn't look away.

"I didn't do anything." The words came out in a halting squeak, and she began to blubber. Sally's eyes stayed fixed for a moment. The police car pulled over to the side. Sally drove past slowly. All they could see through the trees were the two large trucks with sides opened up and spilling their fat hoses on the ground like guts. There were no flames or great arcs of water raining down, just a dome of bright white light and idling trucks. A man in firefighting gear stepped out from behind and motioned for them to stay back, keep away. Sally rolled down the window and put her head out. "Ronnie!" she called, then opened the door and stepped out. The man looked at the ground and shook his head, wiping his brow with a rag in his hand. "Can't go down there, Sally," he said.

"Is it totaled?" Sally asked.

The man was big and had a brushy mustache. Maisie recognized him from the gas station in New Gretna. Sally had talked to him once as they were filling up. She could tell by the way he patted Sally's shoulder and started walking away that the news was very bad.

Alden was on the porch. The headlights swept over him as Sally came down the drive. He was sitting slumped, feet straight out and both arms on the armrests of the chair with the pokey springs and loose stuffing. His bicycle was propped against the corner post of the porch, still loaded down with all his things. Sally marched toward the house, saying "God almighty, Alden." Maisie stood alone in the yard. Alden didn't shift or move a muscle, didn't seem really to have noticed Sally or be paying attention to what she was saying to him, slapping her sides in exasperation. As Maisie approached he came forward in the chair and beckoned to her. A hard lump came into her throat, and her chin began to quiver. He beckoned to her again, and when she came within reach he pulled her toward him and hugged her tightly and whispered.

"I didn't know where you were."

two

At the traffic light Maisie kept her foot on the brake and waited. A miracle. No honking horns. Or she couldn't hear them over the rain drumming on the roof. The wipers slashed back and forth. The light turned yellow, then red again, and still no horns. She took her hands from the wheel and rested them in her lap. It felt oddly calm inside the roaring metal box. Then it was time to go again, and she couldn't. The driver behind her honked once, then again, then angrily leaned on the horn. She turned on her emergency flashers and drove onto the shoulder beyond the intersection. The cars passed, a line of red taillights floating away, shedding and parting the water as if it were a momentary inconvenience. A shard of light cracked across the sky. The thunderclap that followed startled her. She glanced at the GPS—still in touch with the necessary satellites circulating, calculating, reckoning her position from overhead. Cars streamed past, but rather than drive on, Maisie cut the engine and sat in a silence broken only by the tick tick tick of the emergency flashers, against which her own breathing sounded sealed up, sealed in, nested in another space like a Chinese box. She slid the driver's seat back, slipped off her damp espadrilles, tucked her feet up, and sat cross-legged in lotus position. The BMW mandala in the center of the plush steering wheel rose from her lap like a little moon. The wheel was adjustable. She could tilt it up and have more room. But what were millimeters to a roadside Buddha?

The sky brightened, and the storm clouds began to lift. She lowered her window and breathed the asphalt ozone. Even with the window open she felt submerged. In a few minutes cooler, drier air would put a gleam in the atmosphere, and even the flattened weeds sprouting from the cracked pavement would look vigorous and refreshed. Another battery of cars passed. And another. Then there was a pause, and the road was empty for a time. She watched the rain droplets fuse, then stream in rivulets off the car's hood. Another wave of cars collected at the light. Maisie unfolded her legs and started the engine.

She was doing ninety when she passed the port of Elizabeth; SeaLand and Maersk cranes, left; the runways of Newark International on the right. A jet was taking off. She held the wheel tightly, feeling every little detail of the road clicking beneath the tires, the smooth whine of the engine, an amplified connection, slippery and intimate, that could be severed in an instant. When the airplane lifted off she took her foot from the gas. The sudden deceleration was thrilling, though in a different way, something filched, gotten away with. She smiled. It made her happy to be sporty and alert, to do things that middle-aged women simply did not do—reckless, seeking a threshold, a limit. The markers skipped past: 99.8, 99.7, 99.6. She sailed by huge, cake-shaped cylinders, pipes and high-tension power lines, gas turbines—and blinking billboards advertising escapes and diversions from all of it. There was no way to be moving through it except quickly and alone.

"You remember me, Maisie?"

"Of course I remember you, Sally."

"I'm an old woman now." The chuckle that followed didn't seem old at all, but wry and friendly.

"Do you still live in the same house?"

"Not hardly. I'm in a place called Ocean Manor in Manahawkin." Another chuckle and a pause to catch her breath. "It's assisted living, but I get around just fine. How old are you now, honey?" She repeated Maisie's answer. "Fifty-three. My, my." Then, reverting to old auntie, she added, "I bet you're just prettier than ever, too, aren't you?"

"Where is Manahawkin?"

"Between Barnegat and Tuckerton. We went to the beach there. Remember?"

"It's a little fuzzy. It was a long time ago."

Sally laughed. "Maybe to you, honey. To me it all seems like just yesterday."

Her GPS began alerting her to the upcoming exit for the Garden State Parkway. She turned it off and passed Metuchen, Perth Amboy, acres of warehouse, New Brunswick—which she approached in a daydream of winking red lights and a vague sense of harmony with everything in motion, speeding toward her and, flit, flit, flit, vanishing into her mirrors. She pulled off at the Molly Pitcher service area. It no longer fit her memory of the small, fenced lot and picnic area with benches and trees. She parked at the far corner and watched for a while. How many nights had they spent on this acre of asphalt? It was unrecognizable. There was nothing familiar or cozy or civic about any it, just empty, disused picnic tables, brutal concrete affairs, not the green wooden benches initialed with pocket knives and families unfurling out of station wagons. What had Alden called it? A no-place? A non-place?

Outside the service area a young woman in a headscarf was selling sunglasses from a cart and talking loudly on a cell phone. New Jersey Urdu. Maisie paused to look over the selection. The woman smiled, gestured with her free hand, and continued her conversation. Maisie tried on a pair and then another, each time looking at herself in a mirror mounted in the center of the cart. When she put on the third pair the woman cupped the phone and said. "They're to-tally the ones," and resumed her conversation. "No, Ma. No. I'm telling you. It's like ek ghantaa. Nahin. Ek ghantaa!"

Maisie went inside. The Polaroid tint lent a chill to the condensed bustle. On the wall was a large map of the state. She studied it as people hurried in and out of the restrooms, dodging orange cones and yellow signs warning of wet floors, queued up at Starbucks and Roy Rogers and Cinnabon.

Back on the highway, she felt more comfortable. The sunglasses muted the glare. Traffic seemed a little slower south of the Hightstown Freehold exit. At Bordentown she left the turnpike and found herself on a road that was familiar without being in any way distinct. The GPS remained off. She wanted to home in spontaneously, to know when she saw it. She followed the road southward past vigorless subdivisions set down on the flattened landscape. They did interfere with the little she could remember of it, but it was pointless to resent them. When she saw the Carranza Road sign, she braked hard and pulled onto the shoulder. She got out to stretch her legs. If there was anything to recognize, it meant little now. She walked a short distance down the road. Gravelly and familiar. But only slightly. A breeze rustled in the trees. A fine, clear, October day. Her shiny car looked out of place. She felt exposed standing there, brand-new sunglasses, hands in her pockets, just down from where?

She got back in the car and drove on. The colors of the sky seemed to darken and match the deeper greens of heather, cedar, and pine. She remembered a tower and a clear night and more stars than she'd ever seen before. And the name of the road, Carranza. They'd planted mirrors in the dirt. Alden had a whole box of them. Maisie helped set each one on the ground. When they were finished he took her back to Opa and Yva. They didn't seem surprised or upset or angry. Alden hugged her tightly before leaving. He smelled like burned paper and had on the thick black-framed glasses that he wore only when he was driving. Yva asked him to stay for dinner, but he said he couldn't. She couldn't recall him saying good-bye or promising anything. It was possible he said something like "See you later."

She stopped again at a sign that said "Hampton Gate," got out of the car, and walked along a narrow trail that meandered and by its very waywardness actually seemed to be leading someplace. She followed it, trying to recognize features and details in that casual way of knowing oneself to be out of place but also appreciating being there. Were these huckleberries? Was that mountain laurel? Poison ivy? She came to an open clearing. The ground, sandy white, was rutted with tracks. Fallen trees and uprooted bushes had been dragged and dumped at the perimeter. She walked into the center of the clearing over deep ruts and ridges. There wasn't any purpose or sense in the torn-up ground, just empty Budweiser cans and McDonald's wrappers. The sun was high, the air warm and humid. Her shoes were caked. She was heating up uncomfortably and looked for a place to sit but saw nothing even remotely inviting. She returned to the car, turned on the GPS, and drove very slowly on the loose-packed sand. The ruts grew deeper and the road more precarious. It was thrilling to be so lost and yet know precisely where she was. She came to a paved crossing and made a left. A few minutes later she turned right, and, suddenly, she was there. It was a different sort of quiet than the ground-out abandonment of the place she'd just been. The quiet here was of a spark gone out. Alden had read the inscription to her in Spanish. Aviator Captain Emilio Carranza, who died on July 13, 1928, on his goodwill flight. The carving was familiar, too, a plummeting Aztec bird. She circled the monument, scuffing along in the pine needles for shards of mirror that might still be there. How many had they planted? She couldn't recall. It had seemed like many. She sat down and rested against the cool stone of the monument—exactly what they'd done back then.

OCEAN MANOR WAS a sprawling subdivision carved out of pine scrub set down on Route 72 behind a box-store multiplex and a massive Walmart where Maisie ran in to buy flowers. She parked near the entrance and sat for a minute to gather her thoughts. There was something familiar in the slant of the afternoon light, the touch of salt in the air, and tromping around in the woods had made her feel somehow tied in, connected. But still it all felt flat, like anywhere, a little disappointing.

She was taken to Sally's apartment by a cheerful "associate" named Amber. Sally, shrunken and thin in an old print dress and slippers, was waiting at the door. They regarded each other for a moment; then she touched Maisie's forearm. "I don't know whether to laugh or cry." There was a slight tremble. "I'm getting over a cold. Excuse me if I start wheezing."

The place wasn't much more than a hotel room with a bed, an easy chair, a small table and chairs. A sliding glass door led onto a small balcony. Another door with an oversized levered handle led into a bathroom. Sally took the flowers from Maisie and smelled them. "They're beautiful. Thank you."

"Do you have a vase?"

Sally pointed to a glass jar on a shelf and sat down in the

easy chair by the window. Maisie rinsed and filled the jar in the bathroom, then set it on the little eating table. "How long have you been here?"

"Longer than I ever thought I'd live to." Her hair was completely white and pulled into a thin ponytail that hung down to the small of her back. It seemed a lot of hair for an old woman to have, a final possession. "I had a bigger unit with a separate bedroom and a kitchen when I first got here," she said and began talking about Ronnie, a fireman she'd married who was also a carpenter and wood carver and who had died suddenly at the age of seventy-seven. "That's when I sold the house and moved in here. What kind of work do you do, honey? I don't guess you're a housewife."

"What makes you say that?"

"Not too many women are these days. Plus you don't look like one."

"I should say thank you, I guess."

"Do you have a husband?"

Maisie shook her head. "Been divorced four years."

Sally reached for Maisie's hand and held it. "These are working hands."

"I make pots," Maisie said. "I'm a potter."

"A potter! My goodness. Can you make a living with that?"

"Not much of one, I'm afraid. But I'm comfortable enough."

"I supported Ronnie when he lost his job and started carvin'." She let go of Maisie's hand and pointed to a shelf of ducks across the room. "'Course I'll never sell 'em. Been lucky so far—haven't had to. You get good money for your pots?"

"I cover expenses. I also teach at a local college."

"A college teacher!"

"Community college."

"I always wanted to be a teacher," Sally said, pushing up on the arms of the chair as if raising herself, then giving up and sinking back again.

"Can I get you something?"

"No, dear." She shook her head and gave a tired wave. She shifted a little, leaning to one side with hands folded in her lap. It was clearly an effort and made an elegant impression. The door to the balcony was slightly open. A draft stirred the curtain.

Maisie pulled up a chair, and they sat looking at one another in trembling disquiet. When Maisie began to cry Sally touched her on the knee, then removed her hand. There was no track, no course for them to follow. There were no mutual obligations, no bonds or supports. It was hard to balance all the distance and the void between them with a caring Maisie wasn't sure about. There was too much that wasn't clear. Mexico was far away. All she knew was that Alden had died there.

"I had letters and documents explaining everything, all the circumstances," Sally said. "Then I got this letter from a lawyer saying your grandpa and grandma wanted no further contact and would get a restraining order if they had to. Bang. Just like that."

Maisie took it in as if it were someone else they were talking about, another life that had nothing to do with her or with anyone she knew. "When did it happen, Sally?"

"July 20, 1973," the older woman said and looked away.

Maisie repeated the date, trying to match it to something she could recall, but came up blank. Then, as if on cue, she flashed hot, and her heart began to race. Flushed and sweating, she excused herself to go and stand on the balcony. A man in a wheelchair was sitting in front of a gazebo in a patch of lawn between the buildings. He was feeding crumbs to a small flock of sparrows and starlings hopping all around him in the grass. A seagull perched on top of the gazebo cocked its head this way and that. Maisie waited to see if it would launch itself, scatter the smaller birds, and take the crumbs. She wondered if she'd been summoned here to settle something, not necessarily to put things right. A restraining order? The hostility was shameful. It was difficult for Maisie to know what to ask now and even harder to know what she wanted to know.

When she returned inside, Sally pointed to a large box by the door. "I want you to have that," she said. "Don't be disappointed when you open it. It isn't a family album or anything precious like that." She said so with a pained, elderly sarcasm that was then immediately waved away. "Ronnie and I went down there to get Alden's things, and that's all there was. Just his camper and that box."

Maisie nodded.

"It was two weeks before we got down there," Sally continued. "Lord, was that ever something. The middle of the jungle."

"You went to Mexico?"

"No. It wasn't Mexico. It was Guatemala. The middle of nowhere. They had Alden's stuff all locked up in the camper. You remember that camper?"

"Who did?"

"Whadya call 'em. The archaeologists. Went up in a plane they had." A vague look came over her. "It took nearly a week to find them. The middle of the jungle. It caused all sorts of trouble. The government down there. Fellas from the embassy." Maisie watched her struggle with the memory. She didn't know how to join what Sally was telling her to the absence in her heart. One didn't fill such a void with details. But she didn't know what else to put there.

There was a knock at the door, and a housekeeper came in to see if any tidying was necessary. Sally told her to come back, then changed her mind and said there was some trouble with the sink in the bathroom. When the woman went to look Sally became suddenly irritated and told her to come back later. Maisie saw it was time to leave. Sally didn't argue and told her in animated detail where she should stay in Beach Haven. They stood in the doorway. Maisie held the heavy box in both arms. Something in the way Sally put a hand on her cheek reminded her of gathering eggs.

SALLY HAD SUGGESTED the Sea Spray Motel "down to" Beach Haven, but when Maisie saw all the off-season "For Rent" signs along Long Beach Avenue, another idea came to her. By nine o'clock she was standing on the deck of a small bungalow looking into a clear night sky, warmed by the sound of the ocean and the giddy feeling of having run away. She slipped off her shoes and followed a path down to the beach. The sand was still warm. The house was nested among a row of similar ones and stood out only because the places on either side were dark. A breeze was blowing.

The air was cool. She walked along picking up shells in the moonlight.

In the morning she woke up to the sound of gulls. The shells she'd gathered were piled in a little mound around the alarm clock on the bedside table. She lay in bed and watched the flocking birds gather on a dune just outside the window; then she dressed and drove to a coffee shop in Surf City. The parking lot bustled with people coming and going—tennis players, runners, surfers, beachcombers. A grey-haired man wearing a green jogging suit and a gold chain held the door for her, morning newspaper pleasantly tucked under his arm. She thanked him and carried her cardboard tray to the car.

On the way back to the house she dialed Sally's number.

"Who?" The voice was uncertain but not unfriendly.

"Maisie. I visited you yesterday, remember?"

There was a pause, and then she brightened. "Oh, yes. Maisie. Are you at the Surf Inn?"

"No. I found a house to rent. Want to come and stay? For a day or two?"

There was no answer.

"Sally? You still there?"

"I haven't been to the shore in years."

"Think it over. I'll come by this afternoon. "

It felt good to be away. Maisie had nothing with her but

the clothes she was wearing. She'd need a toothbrush, a change of underwear. There were no towels in the bathroom, no sheets on the beds. Back at the house she drank her coffee and fiddled with her phone. There was an Acme less than a mile away. Of course Walmart and Bed Bath & Beyond and Home Depot and Shop Rite and Appleby's and TGI Friday's were all up on Route 72. She stroked and tweezed and pinched and zoomed out on the screen of her iPhone until she was holding the entire matchstick of Long Beach Island in the palm of her hand. What could a person really recall of the past that wasn't veiled or embroidered? What did any fifty-three-year-old remember of being eight? She remembered the fire-truck headlights sweeping across the window. Alden and Sally on the porch talking in low voices. The smell of Tareytons. She wanted to go sit with them. But she was afraid. "Do you have any money?" she heard Sally ask but didn't hear what Alden said, could only imagine him there with legs straight out, hands in his pockets, looking at his feet. She remembered him standing at the sink, washing his dish the next day. "Morning, Maisie," he said the way he did every morning. He dried and put away the dish. "I'm taking you back to your Grandma and Grandpop today."

"Did everything get burned up?" she asked.

"Yes," he said. It wasn't an accusing tone. Just a finality.

"Can I see?"

Alden regarded her for a moment, then said, "C'mon. Get dressed."

Duchamp was parked in the middle of the yard. Alden must have driven him over sometime during the night. Maisie hadn't heard anything. "It's a miracle," Sally said. She brushed her fingertips along the side door, which Alden had opened. Duchamp was dusted with a fine layer of soot. The charred smell grew stronger as they walked up the drive. At the top they could see everything. The sun shone orange on the blackened stumps and piles of char. They approached the ruin without speaking. The bog was open to a view through a wide clearing where the house had stood. The firemen had taken down trees and cleared brush. The area was not just charred and stumpy but strewn with a sprinkling of sand that glittered. She expected to see everything smoldering, but the place had been thoroughly soaked. All that was left were brick pilings and the blackened tin roof all mangled in a heap. The cast-iron stove lay on its side amid the twisted entrails of its smokestack. There were raked-over mounds of sludge that were the remains of Alden's paintings. Sally hugged herself and began to cry, but Maisie was too awed by the sight. It looked like all the other grown-down places she'd been shown and superior, somehow, to the tar-papered, ramshackle places that survived by just barely getting by. Alden prodded and poked around with the toe of his boot, picked up and examined and tossed back things, and acted as if he were there all alone.

"HOW DID IT happen?" Opa and Yva wanted to know.

Maisie explained that fires happened a lot in the pines and described all the burned parts she'd seen driving through the forest with Sally.

"She drives in the forest?" Opa was impressed.

"The house inside is nice?" Yva wanted to know. "She keeps it up all alone?"

"Of course she keeps it up," Opa said.

They wanted to know all about Alden's place and seemed to admire that he was able to live with so little money. "But he refuses to work, and that's no good," Yva said.

Soon they stopped asking or saying anything at all about Alden and Sally. But Alden was all Maisie could think about for a long time. She thought of him often, parked in a corner of some rest area with Duchamp popped up, drinking coffee from his thermos, making notes and sketches.

SALLY WAS WAITING on a bench by the entrance of Ocean Manor with a small bag at her feet. Maisie apologized for being late. "How long have you been sitting out here?" Sally didn't seem to know or care. They went through the sign-out procedure and an involved meds schedule in the main office, then walked out to the car. Sally was smiling. She was still smiling as they turned onto Route 72 and merged into the flow of cars getting off the Garden State Parkway. When they passed the Manahawkin turnoff Sally said, "That's where Ronnie's from."

The place was familiar and unfamiliar and remarkable and forgettable all at the same time, a vacant geography of billboards and signage and moving cars. They came to Manahawkin Bay, and Maisie slowed down at the top of the causeway. The sky was streaked with wisps of cloud, and the horizon was fringed with wetlands broken by the shimmering pastels of bay-front houses and the V-shaped wakes of powerful boats. As they arrived on the sand-and-asphalt commercial strip that was Ship Bottom Sally said, "Did you say you were married? I can't remember."

"We did talk about it a little yesterday, Sally. Divorced. Four years ago. And I have a son in college."

Sally took this in with a blank expression, then turned to look out her window. They continued through the battery of stoplights and surf shops and motels and Realtors and seafood and pizza restaurants. Maisie pulled into the parking lot of a grocery store. "I'm picking up a few things for tonight. Would you like to come in?"

"I'll be just fine, honey. You go on."

"Is there anything you want me to get?"

"Can't think of a single thing."

She parked in the handicapped space near the entrance. "I thought we'd have something simple. How about rotisserie chicken?"

"That sounds wonderful, honey. What is it?"

"You'll see." Maisie smiled and left Sally perched like a little grey bird in the front seat. Inside, she dashed up and down the crowded aisles, stiff and anxious for having taken charge, physical and emotional, and uneasy now for having left Sally alone in the car, so tiny and vulnerable, as she dropped things into her basket—a roasted chicken, carrots, peas, a package of egg noodles, bottled water. Coffee and milk, oatmeal for the morning, and bananas and strawberries. Oh, and a bottle of wine. Yes. She'd said she was recently divorced but hadn't gone into detail. Sally had warned about her tendency to forget things, "Don't take it personally," she said with a smile. "I sure don't." Then, as if peering one-eyed through some telescope pointed out into the universe, she began talking about the day Alden departed on his trip—June 2, 1972—claiming it was also the day the Passamaquoddy and Penobscot Indian tribes filed their landmark land claim suit against the State of Maine. "Joint Tribal Council of the Passamaquoddy Tribe v. Morton—I've studied that decision. Know the whole goddamned thing," Sally said, beaming. Then she launched into a winding description of Ronnie's job maintaining the wooden roller coasters at Six Flags.

A cake! Maisie raced to the bakery counter. Yellow cake with chocolate frosting seemed right, a kiddie birthday cake, and candles would make it perfect, the trick kind that keep relighting and relighting. Sally would like that. Returning to the car Maisie felt giddy, and she secreted the cake in the trunk. With an uncertain glance at Alden's box, she closed the trunk gently. The soft click of the latch was as satisfying as any in the long catalog of attentions she'd paid over the years to subtle little efforts with large, dramatic consequences. She thought about the green-and-white camper, parked with the top popped, Alden working at his drawings on some splintery picnic table. For so long she'd dreamed of finding him by following the great circle line that passed directly through her bedroom; as a high school project she'd taught herself how to calculate geographical distances using ellipsoidal geometry. How had she come upon that? her friends wanted to know when she won the senior project math prize.

EVENING CAME FAST. Sally laughed and laughed at the trick candles on the cake. Maisie felt oddly, quietly shaken. After dinner they sat on the deck in foldout lounge chairs, enjoying the fresh air, the sound of the surf. Sally looked puzzled when Maisie suggested having a look in the box.

"What box?"

"You forgot you gave it to me," Maisie teased.

"Well, yes. I suppose I did."

"Do you remember the gun you used to keep in the drawer by your bed?"

"My pistol?"

"I found it one day when I was snooping in your bedroom."

Sally's arms were crossed. Holding her elbows, ponytail slung over her shoulder, she looked like something out of a Walker Evans photograph. "Don't tell me you played with it!"

"No. But I was tempted to."

Sally shook her head. "Ronnie made me get rid of it when we got married. Said I didn't need a pistol since I wasn't living alone anymore. He had a duck gun and a deer rifle, even though he'd already stopped hunting. Now I don't remember what we did with them." She fell silent, then looked up at Maisie and said, "We didn't ever have children together. No family or anything. But Ronnie was very proud of the way he took care of me. And I loved him for that."

They lay in the chairs gazing up at the darkening sky. "He started carving ducks when he stopped hunting." She paused to consider, then shook her head. "No. That's not right. First he started carving and then stopped hunting. Stopped shooting 'em when he began looking at 'em up real close." She chuckled. "Ronnie's ducks got pretty popular. Hunters started buying 'em up as fast as he could carve 'em. Used to joke that it was lose-lose for the ducks whether Ronnie was hunting or just carving 'em."

"Are those ducks on the shelf by Ronnie?"

"Most of 'em. You bet."

A breeze picked up. Maisie went inside to find some blankets. She shook them over the railing and draped one over Sally's legs. "This isn't your house, is it?" Sally asked.

"No, it isn't," Maisie said.

"Where do you live?"

"Montclair, up in Essex County."

"Alone?"

Maisie nodded. "My son, Karl, started college this year."

"I had a dog."

"Yes. I know. Fish." Maisie smiled, suddenly remembering. The moon was just a sliver on the horizon, and the tide was out. She thought of the connection between moon and tide, of forces exerted by distant bodies on timescales of hours, days, years.

"Did you ever have anyone special besides your husband?" Sally turned to her, pulling the blanket up around her shoulders.

Maisie felt her cheeks flush and immediately understood it wasn't a question but a confession and that it would dim and evaporate quickly in the synaptic ether and be gone. But she answered anyway.

"I was married for twenty-two years," she said. "The last five or six unhappily. It wasn't easy, but we finally went our separate ways. It was pretty mutual in the end."

"Did he cheat on you?"

Maisie shook her head. "Nothing like that."

"Then what happened?"

"I outgrew him." She turned to Sally, realizing how arrogant it sounded. But it was true. She considered how to qualify it—a way of putting it that didn't cast Don as some kind of snail to her—her what?

"You loved him once." Sally was still holding the blanket at her throat, not asking but telling—all over again and also for the very first time.

"Not the way you loved Ronnie, maybe. But it was love."

Maisie left it there, a little surprised at how true and good what she was telling the old woman felt.

"I remember you were very independent as a little girl," Sally said. "I felt bad leaving you alone all day. But you seemed perfectly happy and never complained."

Maisie looked away. There was a halo around the moon and the air felt damp and it felt secluded underneath the wide-open landscape of the night sky. "I wish I could re-member more," she finally said.

Later, unable to fall sleep, she lay in bed listening to the surf in the distance. Sally was in the next room. Maisie had gone in to say good-night and found her propped up by pillows, a glass of water and a battery of prescription bottles on the bedside table. She'd taken out her dentures, undone her ponytail. How close to the grave she looked, without teeth, lipless, hair falling over her shoulders. Maisie kissed the top of her head. Would she know where she was in the morning? What is it like to confront every day like a stranger? Or does one just move like a vagabond through the world feeling entirely independent of it? Day to day, place to place? Without teeth, does it feel like hour to hour?

It was grey dawn when Maisie woke up. She got out of bed and tiptoed out to the deck. A jogger bounded into view, following a path through the shallow dunes down to the water. A gleamless morning damp, without foreground or background. Maisie's memory resembled this flattened view, as if it were, say, October 6, 1981, or January 10, 1975. The dates were no more or less distinct than any others. What had she been doing at fifteen or twenty-one? There were settings, large and small, scatterings associated with states of feeling. Few were as vivid as standing at the window of a West Village restaurant on a bright, sunny morning listening to a band playing the Sunday brunch inside. The music had drawn her, a woman playing an electric violin. When she finished her solo, she turned and beckoned Maisie to come inside. Embarrassed, Maisie hurried off. The streets were quiet. The sun was warm. And now, standing here on a beachside deck, why could she recall that one moment so well—even the names of the players on the chalkboard set out on the sidewalk? Urbaniak, Dudziak. Why so vivid while the rest of her years were a dim and dusky disorder? Submerged, crystallized.

Now the sun was up, and people were beginning to appear on the beach, swimmers, joggers. She went inside, leaving the sliding door open. The house, all light wood and beachy pastels, felt conventional, airy and fresh. She set the coffee machine to gurgle on the kitchen counter and sat on the floor to begin looking through Alden's box, determined not to succumb to that rheumatism of spirit that makes an aching effort of every little thing. Then Sally appeared, completely dressed, hair freshly gathered into a ponytail, teeth in place. Maisie saw right away that she was confused. Sally made her way over to the sliding door.

"Best time for surf fishing is in the morning," she said and gripped the door frame, steadying herself before stepping outside. Maisie slid the box to a corner of the room, imagining Sally and Ronnie at the water's edge together, all leathery and sunburned, wearing baggy tank tops, casting and reeling in their lines. She put out breakfast bowls and cups, poured herself some coffee, and went outside.

"I can't walk on it anymore," Sally said. "Too old for sand."

"At least we have a nice view." Maisie unfolded two chairs and set them side by side. They sat down, but the sun was too bright, and they were forced back into the house after just a few minutes.

They ate breakfast without talking. Sally spooned her oatmeal in deliberate little bites between sips of milky coffee. Maisie wasn't sure if the old woman's silence was lingering confusion or disorientation; then she realized that morning quiet was all that remained of having come first for someone all those years, that Sally was just lagging in place, all alone. "Shall we go for a drive?" Maisie asked as they were finishing. "Have a look at the old house? I'd love to see it again."

Sally shook her head. "It's gone. The state took it over."

"Took it over?"

"They gave me money for it." Her face colored.

"They forced you out?"

"No. They said I could stay there long as I wanted. Just couldn't do anything to it or change anything. There wasn't anybody that wanted it but the state. They said they were protecting it! Happened to lots of people."

"Happened when?"

"A little while back. Nineteen seventy-eight is when they passed the law. Ronnie and I lived there for a few years after that. Then we moved up to Freehold so Ronnie could be closer to work."

Maisie resumed her search through the box and took out a manila folder with notes and Mylar sheets. She showed them to Sally, who nodded and said, "That's the Jetport," as if it were the freshest, uppermost thing in her mind.

"Jetport?"

"It's all in there. A supersonic airport right here in south Jersey." She chuckled and shook her head. "Can you imagine!"

"Something Alden was involved in?" Maisie asked.

"No," Sally said. "He just had his own ideas for what it ought to be."

"When was the last time you looked at any of this?"

"A while ago, honey. It's all the things he was working on after he stopped painting."

Maisie set down the folder. "Alden stopped painting?"

Sally smiled, fully awake and alert all of a sudden. It was as though some inner switch had been turned on. She twisted the end of her ponytail, focused and clear—even her eyes. Then she began to talk about Alden's move to New York. Suddenly he had resources, she said, was busier than he'd ever been. He said he didn't want to paint any-more. He wanted to make landscapes with rocks and dirt. "Put things out there for people to come across," Sally said. "The more remote, the better. He used to say coming across something in the middle of nowhere gets a person to seeing differently."

Maisie glanced at the piles on the floor around her. Sal-ly's sudden snap of energy and clarity was strange. Was it medication? Or a cycling, normal state? She went into the kitchen, poured herself a glass of water, and returned with one for Sally, who took it with both hands and held it in her lap. The room was now bright with morning sun. Too bright. Maisie adjusted the blinds and stood in the sliding doorway looking down toward the beach. The air shim-mered. The people walking in the surf seemed scaled to an entirely different order. A large gull flew over the house, banked abruptly, and landed on the rim of a trash barrel. It perched for a moment, cocking its head in that expectant bird way, then opened its wings, fell back onto the breeze, and flew away.

Sally held the water glass in her lap. Then she began to talk about a man named Ed Andrews who once lived in Egg Harbor, a fiddler who'd taught himself to play in spite of a strict Quaker upbringing. "He liked to sit out on his porch on Sundays, and anyone who wanted could drop by. Ed was a bit of a drinker and knew how to have a good time. Then one day he was plowing his field and turned up a human skull. An Indian, the story goes. But I don't know how they'd have been able to tell that."

Maisie slid the door closed, sealing out the warm air and the rushing sound of outdoors with a rubbery slurp.

"The skull got him thinking. And it wasn't long before he got rid of his fiddle—smashed it up, threw it into the river—and then he started reading the Bible and thinking deep thoughts. Pretty soon Ed was preaching. People came from all over to hear him."

"When are we talking about?"

"Oh, I don't know. Two hundred years ago, maybe," Sally said. She paused, seemed to drift.

Maisie didn't quite know what the point had been.

That it was an old tale seemed important. She wasn't sure whether she should risk asking where the story came from or just leave Sally to meander.

"It's about giving up," Sally said. Her voice changed entirely, and she focused her eyes on some middle distance between them as if reciting things memorized long ago. She started with the house and land she'd given up. That was the expression she used. Given up. It wasn't a term of surrender, she explained. "It was a sacrifice. A sacrifice!" She repeated the word in an odd, incantatory way that mixed rumination with righteous emotion and a dash of pulpit oratory. Then she began talking about the Swedes and Finns who had settled on land that was home to the Lenni-Lanape Indians; and then about Peter Stuyvesant, who sailed up the Delaware River in 1655 with seven hundred men, took what the settlers had been calling New Sweden, and renamed it New Amstel. Nine years later England took it from the Dutch. This, she explained, was the second time it had been given up—the first having been on the part of the Lenni-Lanape, and then the Dutch. "They both sacrificed. The Indians and the Dutch. That was very important to us."

"Us?"

"Ronnie and me and the folks who were trying to figure out what to do."

"About what?"

"The Pinelands Act. They took our land to make the Pinelands National Reserve."

"Who did?"

"The U.S. Congress and the State of New Jersey."

Maisie glanced at her, slightly skeptical. "Is that right? I had no idea."

"That was the trouble. Nobody knew or cared. Wasn't much we could do about it anyway. Mostly we were just trying to figure out how the land around here started changing hands." She fell briefly quiet, then resumed her thread, explaining that Charles II of England took from the Dutch all the land between the Delaware and Connecticut Rivers to the upper reaches of the Hudson River and gave it to his great good friend the Duke of York, who turned right around and gave most of it to his great good friends, Sir George Carteret, treasurer of the Royal Navy, and John Berkeley, First Baron of Stratton, calling it New Jersey in honor of Carteret's loyal defense of the Isle of Jersey against the Parliamentarians during the English Civil War. But then, much to the distress of the Duke of York, Berkeley sold his share to a man named John Fenwick, who turned around and sold it to four of his Quaker brethren, one of whom was William Penn. "And then a quintipartite deed was drawn up dividing New Jersey into two provinces, East and West."

"Quintipartite?" Maisie interrupted, charmed by Sally's deliberate pronunciation.

"Quintipartite," the old woman repeated and went on with her story. She said a division line was drawn in 1676. "The Keith Line, after George Keith, who finally did the actual perambulation." She glanced at Maisie. "It's the traditional English word for setting boundaries. By walking. Don't you love that?"

Sally got up and shuffled to the sink for another glass of water, explaining as she refilled her glass how the line was the basis for drawing boundaries until 1743, when a man named John Lawrence surveyed yet another line that ran one hundred and fifteen miles from Little Egg Harbor to the Delaware River. "And there's where it ended, honey, at a nice old elm tree growing out of a bushy gully." She put her glass in the sink and leaned against the counter, bracing herself with both hands for support. "The one hundred fourteen mile marker was a forked white oak. Hundred thirteen was a pine; hundred twelve was Spanish oak growing on the north side of Pahaqualin Mountain."

She continued talking as Maisie helped her back to the sofa and with rising passion explained that the boundaries of her family's property had also been marked by trees, that it had been a common and accepted practice all across the region. "And you know what, honey? Maybe trees are exactly right. They live long but not too long, and then it's somebody else's turn. I'd be all for that. Just not the goddamn government! They took it from us just like the English took it from the Indians. When our trees were all still there! Still healthy, still standing. We knew what we had. We knew the ground we were standing on and just wanted to know the grounds we had for standing on it." Evidently, knowing that the land had been simply taken from the Indians and that the whole subsequent history of its ownership rested on that initial theft made giving it up easier. She thought the Dutch may have felt something similar in surrendering it to the English without firing a shot; or the Lenni-Lanape, whose ideas of property were very likely different and who may not have conceived of land in terms of ownership at all.

"It was just eggs to them," she said.

"To the Indians?" Maisie asked.

"No. To the Swedes and the Dutch. When they first waded through the wetlands the place was filled with millions and millions of nesting birds. There were eggs everywhere. Just laying around. They called it Eyre Haven, Egg Harbor. I think they saw the land the same way, something just lying there, theirs for the taking."

When Sally went quiet for a moment, Maisie stepped out to the deck, opened the umbrella, and arranged the foldout chairs in the shade. There seemed no better way to spend the day than lounging right there, looking out at the ocean. She helped Sally get settled, put a plastic pitcher of ice water and two glasses on the sun-bleached table between them. Sally rubbed her knee and turned her face to the breeze with a look of contentment that was much more than a smile. Then she began a meandering description of the river named after Eric Mullica, a Swede who settled along its banks sometime in the 1690s. Soon afterward, she said, the land began changing hands. "And that's when the Sooy and Leek and Cavileer families all established themselves and began cutting timber and building ships and fishing the bays and forging iron in the bogs."

Keeping up with her became difficult. Maisie closed her eyes and drifted in and out of a dimness she didn't want to pierce. Her own memory was so sketchy. She only vaguely recalled the last time she'd seen Sally. She'd come to New York with the fireman, the man she would marry, unannounced. Maisie was in bed, asleep. She heard Sally's voice and went into the living room. She recognized the fireman right away. Sally hugged her tightly, sniffling and red-eyed. When she woke up the next morning and asked where Sally was Yva said not to worry. Maisie asked why Sally had been crying and Yva said when she was older she'd understand. She asked why she'd brought the fireman. Fireman?

What fireman? Yva asked. Maisie was relieved. She asked about Sally a few more times, but she got more or less the same reply.

And then the years passed.

MAISIE WAS STILL untangling all the disjointed talk of history and property and Indians and eggs the next day. She had wanted to steer the discussion to family and precious things, but the battered old Allied Van Lines box with its guts spilled across the floor acted like a warning. Even though Sally had cautioned her not to see it in those terms, she couldn't imagine any other way to look at it. Nearly fifty years on, even the most meticulously conserved family mementos were just a precious chronicle of wreckage.

Late in the morning she helped Sally into the front seat of her car and turned the air conditioner on full. Then she went back inside and fetched the folders from the box, which Sally had instructed her to bring along. It was a very warm Indian-summer day. Summer houses squatted on empty driveways, one after another, in various states of postseason abandonment. Sally took out what she called her "granny goggles," oversized plastic sunglasses that obscured her entire face. "Didn't used to need them," she apologized, putting them on. "Then I had cataract surgery, and, good Lord, it was like taking down the curtains and throwing the windows open! Everything so clear it hurt!"

They passed through Ship Bottom and drove over the causeway. This time Maisie didn't slow down for the view. They glided along, sealed up in the air conditioning and the faint memory of a noisier ride in the old Willys with flip-flops, snacks, and floppy hats and Sally's Tareytons smoldering in the ashtray. Back on the mainland they turned south and drove past fast-food franchises dispersed among repair shops, appliance stores and shattered signs that stood like links to an era of homier commerce. In Tuckerton they passed a Seaport Museum where large signs advertised an upcoming Baymen's Seafood and Music Festival and The Revenge of the Jersey Devil Murder Mystery Dinner Show. "Is that a real lighthouse?" Maisie asked, pointing to the old colonial building with a copper-roofed heptagon rising from the center of the roof.

"None of it's real, honey. Used to be nothing but woods along the creek here."

They stopped at a traffic light. A black Ford pickup pulled alongside them, throbbing with percussive bass. A heavily tattooed arm hung out the window, a big, meaty banner. When the light turned green and the arm sped off Sally said, "Ronnie used to take me to the fights down in Atlantic City. Bally's, the Tropicana. Ever been to a fight?"

Maisie shook her head. "Never much cared for boxing." It came out a little more priggishly than intended. She conjured an image of the younger Sally and the noise and gleam of colored silk and flying sweat and spit. "Did you bet on them?"

"Not me. But Ronnie did."

Maisie was charmed but didn't quite know why; knew only a few movies and the strange charisma of Mohammed Ali and that trembling Olympic torch lighting with the world seeing one thing and Ali very possibly seeing nothing at all.

"Did you enjoy them?"

"Enjoy what?"

"The fights."

"I suppose I did," Sally said. "Not the fighting. More just being there with Ronnie." She paused, then shook her head. "No. That's not true," she corrected herself. "I just went. It wasn't until after he was gone that I realized I had liked being with him." She turned to Maisie. "Did you say you were married?"

"Divorced." Maisie sighed, getting used to the chutes and ladders.

"Well, when you were married you didn't go around all the time thinking how much you liked being together, did you?"

"No. I suppose I didn't."

"And you don't go around thinking how much you like being divorced all the time, do you?"

Stage Road was paved and ran parallel to the original dirt track, where high-tension power lines were now strung through the forest in a great swath of infrastructure. When they crossed over the Garden State Parkway Maisie turned on the GPS. Sally watched, mildly curious, then returned to looking out her window. "Huckleberries," she said. "In summer those bushes are thick with them." She went quiet for a time then, a few minutes later, said, "Things are just starting to color up. Nothing like it used to. Yellow, red, gold. Swamp maple. Gum. Sassafras. The woods were thicker then."

Maisie squinted at the dashes of color flashing through the pine-needle green. "Do you remember the old stage road?"

"Like the back of my hand, honey. And the pine thickets, and oak and savanna bottom all the way to Shamong and Atsion."

The old road was just visible through the trees, a sandy track that once brought people down from Camden and Philadelphia through pinewood and swampland to the seaports at Tuckerton and Little Egg Harbor. Maisie remembered how it felt to bicycle on the sand, pedaling behind

Alden all loaded down and wobbling. She said so to Sally, who chuckled and nodded. "The bicycling and painting. All that came from Ned Knox."

"Who?"

"Ten trillion tiny elfmen / A mollycule in size / Have taken atom airplanes / And mounted to the skies."

"Go on," Maisie said.

"He always had a new one whenever he came by. Rocks and grass and dirt and trees / All the world is made of these / Our house with all the nails and locks / one time was trees and parts of rocks!" She broke off, shaking her head. "Our parents knew Mr. Knox from way back. He started painting around this area way back before World War I and was already old when we knew him. He'd come around a couple of times a year on his bicycle, in the late fall usually, when the sand was hard and easier to ride on and there was also more to see, more color. He took Alden with him a few times. Alden never wanted to be anything but a painter after that."

Maisie struggled to recall if she'd ever heard the name.

"And what a whirr above they make / who says it is the storm? / ten trillion elfin aeroplanes / are flying in a swarm." She laughed. "The poem is about snowflakes! Alden figured it out. He got so worked up and excited whenever Mr. Knox showed up. He lived up in Toms River, came down here, usually around Thanksgiving, and stayed at Alden's house, then at our house, each for a couple of days, and he'd go off in the woods to paint. Remember the paintings I had in the house back then? They were Ned's."

Maisie felt the tug of something that consoled her. "What happened to him?" she asked.

"Oh, he passed away a long time ago."

"And the paintings?"

"I still have a few of them. Had to sell most of 'em when I moved to Ocean Manor. Didn't have any place for them."

"Did he leave any to Alden?"

"Sure. The ruins of the old Wading River Forge. That was Alden's favorite. I kept that one."

Maisie went quiet for a few minutes. Alden flickered by on his bicycle, slightly different now for what Sally had just told her.

"Do you have any of Alden's paintings, Sally?"

Sally shook her head. "I asked many times. He was funny that way. I never understood it. A shame, too."

"Was he planning to ever come back here to live?"

"I don't know what he had in mind." Then she turned and said, "He wasn't running away from anything, Maisie. He was giving something up."

There was a long silence, and Maisie thought of Alden. Crusty jeans, stubble, worn boots; more simulacrum than memory, more feel than feeling. Maybe he hadn't run away. But he had vanished. From her life, her thoughts—hadn't been driven or banished, just faded and gone.

"What was he giving up?" she finally asked.

Sally coughed, took off her goggles, and wiped her eyes with a tissue she produced from her sleeve. "His place," she said, putting the goggles back on and tucking the tissue up her arm. "Children grow up and move on. People come and go. All we ever have is a place. Not things, not people, but a place. They say you can't take it with you—but you do. Yes, you do. When you go it goes with you. And it's just an emptiness that's left behind."

She flashed a weak smile, clearly exhausted by all the talking. Maisie reached over and patted her arm. They remained quiet until they arrived in Green Bank, where Sally instructed Maisie to turn left at the bridge over the Mullica. They drove past a row of old houses—several of which she pointed to and named the former owners of. At the end of the road they came to an old church standing at the center of a small graveyard.

"What you want to see is in there," Sally said.

Maisie glanced around. "In the church or the grave-yard?"

Sally pointed to the woods. "In there. It's on the map."

Maisie turned off the engine and rolled down the windows. The place was old and sleepy, with gravestones scattered in clusters and a tentative-looking picket fence that leaned over and disappeared altogether in places. The church was a wooden building with a pitched roof and an awning over the front door supported by two wooden posts. There was no steeple. A simple sign under the peaked roof read, "Green Bank M. E. Church."

Maisie opened the door to get out, but Sally stopped her. "You need to know a few things before you go looking." She pointed to a house on the other side of the cemetery. "The Driver House," she called it, after Samuel Driver, who built it and was buried next to it just six years later. The property was, she said, part of a three hundred–acre tract of land surveyed in 1730-something by Issac Pearson. Over the next several generations it passed into and out of the Sooy family, who finally subdivided and sold a portion of it, then mortgaged and lost their remaining acres to the Union National Bank. Then Joseph Wharton, the Philadelphia industrialist and steel baron, acquired it. Wharton bought up nearly one hundred thousand acres of the pinelands to tap into the vast and pristine Kirkwood/Cohansey aquifer and export its waters to Philadelphia, where typhoid was epidemic. His plan was blocked when the State of New Jersey banned the export of water. With that, Wharton lost interest in the entire 100,000 acres, which were finally bought from his heirs by the state in 1954 and turned into the Wharton State Forest. "The Wharton ledgers were very important to our work," Sally said.

They got out of the car. The front of the church faced the river, and Sally pointed to a house across the road, which she called the Old Storehouse. Maisie knew that cargo ships once were built here that sailed up and down the mid-Atlantic coast carrying timber and charcoal and iron and glass to New York, Philadelphia, and even Europe and the West Indies. She asked if the shipyard in Lower Bank was still making boats.

"I remember going with my father to C. P. Leek and Sons to watch the christening of a boat," Sally said. "Leek. Funny name for a boat builder, don't you think?"

"How old were you then?" Maisie asked.

"Guess I must have been fourteen, fifteen." Then she seemed to lose track; took off her goggles and rubbed her eyes. Maisie wondered if it was time to go back to the house for some rest. As she was about to suggest it, Sally turned to her and asked, "Why did your folks cut ties with me the way they did like that? I never did understand it."

A robin was hopping in the grass just a few feet away. Maisie watched the bird and felt something drain from her. She didn't know what to say. The bird hop-hopped this way and that, drawing neither closer nor farther away, paying no attention and yet alert to some secret signal it would immediately react to.

"I think they were afraid," Maisie finally said. How else to put it? What more was there to say? There was nobody alive anymore. It no longer mattered.

"It wasn't like I was going to try and take you away from them," Sally said. Then she smiled and added, "Even if maybe I'd wanted to." She shook her head. "It was cruel, though. No question about that."

"I guess I could say the same of my father," Maisie said.

They continued to watch the bird. Then Sally turned and with a wry smile said, "We're all orphans, honey. At some point along the way."

Maisie didn't want to pursue it. She had never considered herself an orphan. They walked through the graveyard full of Sooys and Weeks and Cramers and Crowleys. Sally had something to say at nearly every headstone. The whole history of Green Bank, of New Jersey itself, was in the ground beneath them. Maisie listened to Sally's heirloom stories, leaping over decades and centuries like puddles. "Have you written any of this down?"

Sally laughed. "People've been coming through here collecting stories for a long time. Father Beck was one of them. He collected everything, family by family. Story by story. His books are famous. When the Pinelands Act was passed the government sent in people to collect everything else—right down to soil and rocks and plants and junk from people's yards. Some of Ronnie's ducks are in a museum down to Washington! Birds he wasn't even done carving. They were happy to take them all. My house and our land, too."

Maisie asked why the graves were all spread around and not organized in family plots.

"Because everyone in here's related in some way or other," Sally answered.

Maisie went to the car and fetched one of the folders she'd taken from Alden's box and a bottle of water, which they passed back and forth sitting on the church step. "My dad would get us pickles from Hattie Ford's store. Straight out of a wooden barrel. We'd set right here eating 'em. Alden, too."

Maisie had to work at separating the nostalgia Sally was trying to evoke from all the clichés of small-town America. It wasn't possible. The images were too firmly engrained. She couldn't ignore them, and that troubled her. Being so wise to also made her feel emptied of something.

A van pulled up in front of the Old Storehouse across the way. R & B Heating and Cooling. It was a private residence now, renovated, climate controlled, with double-glazed windows and a new Toyota in the driveway. "Do you know who lives there?" Maisie asked.

"Not anymore," Sally said.

The repairman got out and waved. Maisie waved back. A sudden breeze picked up. The sound of a lawnmower beat back the shadows of Sally's reminiscences. "You miss the past, don't you? The good old days," Maisie said.

"Miss them?" Sally answered right away. "I live in them. Quite comfortably, thank you." Her hand shook as she held the water bottle to her mouth to drink. "It's the goddamn present I have trouble with!" She wiped her chin with the back of her hand.

"How far are we from your old place?"

"Right in there." She pointed to the woods. "About a mile in."

Maisie took this in. "I always thought your place was far away from everything."

"It is. I mean it was. In a way. None of it's there anymore, though."

"I also never realized we were so close to the river. Did we ever come this way?"

"I reckon we must've."

"Was Alden's place in there, too?"

"Go on in; have a look. But don't waste time trying to

find the old place. Have a look at where Alden put his city."
She pointed to the folder Maisie had brought with them.

"His city?"

"Right in there." She nodded to the woods. "Down to
the river. He wanted to put something there that would
grow up, not down."

The folder contained old maps and sheaves of drawings
and notes. The oldest document looked like a fragment of
a very old map. Maisie carefully slipped it from the folder
and held it in her lap.

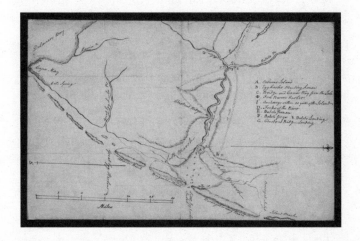

"That was ours." Sally stroked the map surface as if
somehow coming into contact with the land itself. "It's
parkland now," she said. "Remember Alden's friend Roy?"
she asked and pointed to the name I. Cramer.

Maisie shook her head.

"Roy Cramer. His house burned down that summer you were here, too. He had an old Willys just like mine. Kept mine running for years—well, sort of. Finally bought it off me for parts. Granny Cramer was his mother. She could remember when they were still building three-masted ships here and driving coal boxes out of the woods with mules and making paper up in Harrisville. She's buried right over there." She pointed to a corner of the graveyard. "Roy's over there, too."

Maisie was reminded for some reason of the stretch of the Garden State Parkway that runs directly through the Holy Sepulchre cemetery in East Orange. She thought of the sprawling graves on either side of the busy highway, how the generations continue to buzz over and pile on top of one another in most places, though here the buzzing and piling has ceased and the dead aren't quite so traversed upon.

She set the map aside and spread the strange drawings of Alden's city out on the church stoop.

The one labeled "Chromosome Urbaine" seemed to her the trace of all the living and dying Sally had been talking about. Not only would bodies be buried in his city, but the place would be buried in the bodies of those who had lived

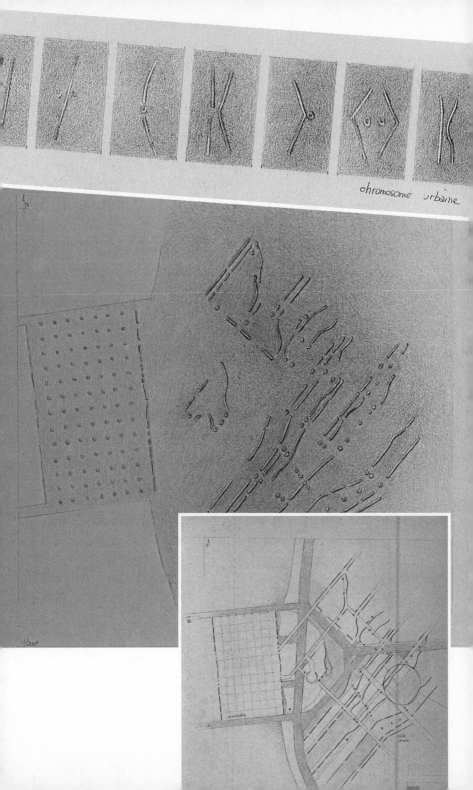

chromosome urbaine

there. I am the place in the world in which I walk, Maisie thought, as though she could hear Alden's voice.

Beside her, Sally was breathing a little heavily. "This isn't the first city anyone ever planned here," she said, closing her eyes and tilting her face to the sun. "Just upriver was a place called Hermann City. Right next to the old Sooy homestead. A man bought the land from the Sooys to build a huge glass factory there and a city for the factory workers." Eyes still closed, she chuckled and shook her head. "The factory got built, a huge eight-potter. And it was shut down the same year. You can walk into the woods along the river now and find absolutely nothing."

Maisie was not sure she wanted Sally to continue. The old woman seemed to be taking such pleasure in all the vanishing. And Maisie didn't feel that way. Not at all. Everything she had in life was tied to a very ordinary house in Montclair, a suburban place that gave her comfort. "I'd like to see the old place," she said. "What it's like now."

"Don't waste your time, honey. It's like nothing was ever there. Besides, you'll never find it."

Maisie returned the drawings to the folder and stood up. They debated whether Maisie should leave her phone or take it. The GPS would be useful, but Sally might want to have it just in case.

"In case of what?" She laughed. "Honey, that phone

ain't gonna save me. Besides, I wouldn't know how to use it. I'll wait for you inside." She pointed to the church.

Maisie helped Sally to her feet. They entered the empty church and walked arm in arm down the aisle. "Like we're getting married," Sally joked. It was cool inside. The wooden floor creaked underfoot. The benches were pushed close together and positioned up near the front. The altar was no larger than an ordinary dining table and covered with a simple white cloth. The air smelled of old wood and oil. Sally chose the first row, in front of the pulpit. "We weren't big churchgoers in our family," she said in a lowered voice. "We were Quakers on my mother's side. And my father was an atheist."

A sobering light streamed in through three tall windows on either side. Sally seemed pensive when Maisie got up to leave.

"I won't be long," she said.

Sally patted her arm. "Take your time, honey. And enjoy the view down to the river."

But it was the old place Maisie wanted—to see it with her own eyes. She studied the map on her phone, then followed the road to where it ended just a few hundred yards beyond the church and became a narrow footpath that led her away from the river and into the woods. In a few minutes the path disappeared entirely. She found a good-sized stick and used it to clear the way, stepping carefully and sweeping low-hanging branches and tangles of vine out of the way. The ground was soft. Sally said there was nothing—but certainly there was something left to see, traces. Chicken wire. An old sofa. Broken bottles and panes of glass.

Mosquitoes swarmed and buzzed. Maisie swatted and wiped them from her forehead, a bloody smear in her palm. The water bottle was nearly empty. She took a few cautious sips, looking for something to recognize. There were oaks and pines and maples just beginning to turn. The underbrush was dense but not impassable. Mountain laurel, greenbriar, huckleberry, poison ivy. Weeks, Leeks, Cavileers, Cramers, Sooys, Van Sants, Mapps. She felt herself beginning to overheat. Her blouse clung to her back; her arms were mottled, flecked and smeared with dirt. The sky had clouded over. There was a someplace in here, and Maisie was going to find it. She pressed on, beating the brush with her stick, pausing here and there to consult her phone, on which she appeared as a blinking dot in a color-corrected field of green. She could see her position relative to church and graveyard, to town and river and county and state and region, a blinking presence in the palm of her hand. A short distance later she came to a wide track that had once been a graded road. A tunnel now, she could see down it a fair distance. It also showed up clearly on her phone, a viridescent stripe in a sea of deeper green. What was she looking for? Sally's place? Or something else? Not a place at all but an emptiness, a void in her memory and her heart.

The road ended suddenly. She could see through the thinning trees, but there was nothing to mark the way. What seemed to be a clearing turned out to be a grove of young pines about half an acre across and under five feet high. It was too dense to enter, and she walked around the perimeter, expecting any moment to come across the collapsed frame of a house or a pile of rusted chicken wire and bricks and masonry that would resolve into a foundation, a hole, something she might recognize.

But there was nothing. At the other side of the thicket she sat down on the trunk of a fallen tree. Her arms trembled as she slipped the pack from her shoulders, thinking how her ex-husband, Don, would have reacted to the situation with mild-mannered chastisements—against which her barreling impulsiveness had always sparked those familiar frictions that had bound them together—until they drove them apart. Twenty-two years. She glanced at her phone. Don would by now be looking at his watch and insisting they turn back. Yes, yes, she would agree, but first just one more this and let's just that, and only when he got pissed off would the turnaround occur—all the better and more rewarding in Maisie's view for having been forestalled and all possibilities exhausted.

She got back to her feet, shouldered the pack, and set off in the direction of the river, picturing to herself the view of the meandering river from high above and the place—a lazy, grassed-over lowland that was the opposite of looking at a watch yet also had to do with waiting, a living vestige of her father's contentment. How happy being there must have made him, and how good it made her feel to be there now, walking. How fresh and unstuck and out of place.

Alden's city—Takokan—was not grown down or grown up but simply a place of possibilities, a matrix from which an inhabited place would arise. The grooves of the drawing were deeply incised into the mat board, then rubbed into relief with pencil. The site was clearly marked on the accompanying map, set down just before the bend where the river turns eastward and widens above Lower Bank. Alden had circled all the cemeteries. Directly next to the Lower Bank bridge he'd written, "Yoos Sooy (1737)" and "John Cavileer (1813)." He'd also placed an X labeled "Eric Mullica" just downriver, above the cemetery marked "Adams and Johnson."

It wasn't clear to Maisie what connection he was making between those sites and the foundations of the city that was to be established upriver from them—unless it was to make reference to the earlier places, all traces of which had slowly disappeared from the landscape Maisie stood in now but whose vestigial DNA would be symbolized in the architectural foundation of the future city. She began to see it. If the living carry the dead in their genes, why not make that trace the basis of an urban geography? Maybe for Alden a chromosomal structure had been somehow truer to the lived dimensions of a place—at least as true as a local tradition like, say, duck carving.

According to the notes Takokan was to be constructed on flowing walls up to fifty feet high and at least three to five feet thick. The surfaces of these colossal edifices would be scored, split open, and even knocked down in places; these gaps and spaces were where people would construct their dwellings, building and incorporating parts of the wall. A series of elevations and floor plans demonstrated a variety of approaches, modern, classical, ancient, and even Neolithic. The drawings seemed nested in both permanence and fragility. Alden's structures would molt and shed and become other structures. Takokan was a place that would be permanent and a ruin at the same time.

Just a few hundred feet into the tall grasses, she came to a clearing where she slipped off her pack and took out Alden's drawings. The ground was slightly higher here, soft and sandy. Not quite a dune but a hummock. Although there were no footprints or tire tracks, it looked as though it had been recently traversed. The riverbank was just a few hundred feet away but inaccessible. In the near distance was a lean-to made of sticks, which she realized was a hunter's blind. A speedboat rounded the bend and skimmed down-river, followed moments later by two Jet Skiers who darted and jumped over its white-capped wake, weaving this way and that in a marauding frenzy, then, turning sharply, sped back upriver.

The air smelled sweet. Sunlight fell just so. Being there was thrilling, like stumbling across the hidden entrance to a cave. She spread the drawings in a semicircle and sat down, crossing her slightly stiff legs, chin cupped in her hand. A so-called Island of Communication was to be located along this section of the river. In the drawings it seemed to be separated from the city by a line of broken walls. It was la-beled the "mind" of the city and laid out in regularly spaced columns that would provide the main supports for places devoted to "governance, administration, places of worship and open to all current and future technologies," a highly rational and rationalized space also referred to in the notes as a "sea-level Acropolis." Maisie suspected the reference, an oxymoron, was meant to call attention to the deliberate vulnerability of the site—not a citadel on a hill but a jetty, open and exposed to the flowing currents of the river and everything on it. In Alden's vision people would move back and forth between it and the "irrational" residential and commercial zones.

Gradually the place began to form itself, blocks laid on the earth, the walls thick, solid, constructed from stone and concrete with foundations deep in the ground. The cracks began to appear in the walls, large and small; then, in the cracks and collapsed walls, the foundations for ruins—Petra, Palenque, Persepolis. Machu Picchu, Mesa Verde, Tintern Abbey, a chromosomal template determining where the walls would and would not be. It was all there. She didn't need to close her eyes to picture it. Not at all. It was possible to introduce something impossible into the world and thereby reveal something entirely new, something very distinct and precise. And her presence there these many years hence among his drawings blew it all into a new dimension. It was not an illusion, and so much more than a fantasy, and possible because the world is simply there to overlook! Up in the sky!

Her legs began to ache. She stood up to stretch and took some pictures with her phone. The jet skiers returned for another bout of wave jumping. From her slightly elevated position she had a view across the marshes along both sides of the river, which widened just around the bend. Grasses and reeds stretched in every direction, waved golden brown in the mid-October light, fringed on the horizon by a thin band of green forest. She imagined this gauzy afternoon light falling on Alden's city, how it would settle in this particular place under this particular dome of sky and add to the blues and greens and yellows. Sally had mentioned an old muskrat trapper named Tom who ran traps in the marshes below Lower Bank and marked his traps by sticks with strips of purple rag tied to them. She'd described how muskrat houses were made up of mounds of swamp grass with tunnel holes at the base that could be as big as a foot in diameter and run as deep as several feet under the mud. No market for muskrat fur anymore, she'd said, which meant that the marsh was probably teeming with them now. Maisie wondered whether Alden's plan for the city had taken into account the invisible cities of wildlife that Takokan would have to share this spot with. She hoped they had. But at the bottom of the final page of notes was written, "I have graven it within the hills and my vengeance upon the dust within the rock—A. Gordon Pym."

Was Takokan a dream or a curse? Maisie's father must have been unsure himself.

SHE SAW THE car through the trees. But it wasn't until she reached the end of the trail that the scene resolved itself.

A police car, "Sheriff's Department" emblazoned on the side, was parked directly in front of the church. She ran, calling "Sally!?" as she bounded up the steps and into the church. There was no one. She glanced about, fluttering, panicked, then saw them through the window and dashed back outside.

Sally was sitting on a gravestone. "Sally!" Maisie checked her pace and marched down a row of headstones toward them. The policeman stood aside as she approached. She touched Sally's shoulder. "Are you all right?"

"She was wandering along the road up by the bridge," the policeman said. "Someone put in a call. I found her sitting here."

"She wanted to wait in the church," Maisie said, catching her breath. "I got a little lost. Oh, Sally. I'm so sorry."

"You a relation?" the policeman asked.

"She's my aunt." Maisie stroked Sally's shoulder. "It's me, Sally. I'm back now. It's okay. Everything's all right." Then she turned to the policeman. "It's my fault. I shouldn't have left her."

The man looked away. Tubby, clean-shaven, wearing a well-pressed uniform, a gun, and masses of gear hanging from his belt.

"She was fine when I left her. Really. Totally fine."

"Teddy's brother played drums," Sally said.

Maisie crouched in front of Sally. "We're going home now, Sally. I'm going to take you home, okay?"

"You want me to call for some assistance?" the officer asked, placing a hand on his belt.

"I don't think that's necessary, Officer. She's just a little disoriented."

"How far do you have to go?"

"Joe Ware's vegetable crates and hamper lids were all made from cedar." Sally pointed toward the woods and smiled at Maisie and the officer. "Trees taken right in there and milled at Bozarth's down to New Gretna." Then she looked at the officer. "Bill Parker was the Burlington County sheriff back then. Remember Bill Parker?"

The officer shook his head, unsmiling.

"She's from here, Officer," Maisie explained. "Family goes way back. Owned property back in there." She nodded in the direction of the forest.

"She couldn't tell me her name," the officer said. "Or where she lives."

Maisie looked at the gravestone Sally had been sitting on and nodded. Jesse Alfred Sooy, 1843–1864.

"That your car back there?"

Maisie nodded.

"Were the church doors open when you got here?"

"Yes, they were," Maisie answered, a little alarmed and not sure what the point of the question was.

"I'm gonna need to check your driver's license and registration," he said and walked ahead, all jangling gear and squeaking leather.

Maisie took Sally's elbow and started back to the car. She settled the old woman in the front seat and rummaged in the glove box for the registration, which she handed over along with her driver's license. "Thank you, Officer," she said. "Sorry again for the trouble."

In the car Sally was mostly silent. Maisie's eyes crept over again and again. Sally looked out the window, contented.

"You were right," Maisie finally said. "I looked and looked and couldn't find anything. Not a trace. But I did find Alden's city."

"Aserdaten?"

"Alden's city."

"Aserdaten. Nobody knows for sure if it was ever there at all."

"Aserdaten?"

"Asa Dayton," she pronounced slowly. "Asa. Dayton. Mr. Knox thought maybe it was the man's name. From Isaiah. Israel. Izzy. Then just Asa. Reverend Beck tried to find it, too. Him and Mr. Knox together. I don't believe they ever got there, even though it showed up on all the old maps. A real place, once." Sally looked down into her lap, smiling to herself, and then began a rambling list of other places—the Forked River Mountains, Webb's Mill, and finally Aserdaten again—a man, she said, who had imported and kept red-tailed deer—for food?—she wasn't sure. "They ruined all the small farms when they escaped and spread all over the area. Rocks and grass and dirt and trees / All the world is made of these / Our house with all the nails and locks / one time was trees and parts of rocks!"

And that was it. All the meticulously remembered detail Sally had recalled over the past two days had collapsed, become scrambled. What, Maisie wondered, had happened?

When they arrived back at Ocean Manor Sally turned to her. "Thank you, honey," she said and got out of the car as if for the hundredth time. It wasn't Amber at the front desk but someone else. Maisie's hand shook as she signed the register, handed over the plastic bag of meds. Sally insisted on carrying her battered little valise from the car.

"She's a little disoriented," Maisie apologized.

Everybody knew just what to do and sprang into action. Sally's designated care manager, Terry, was already in the apartment, no-nonsense, ready to take over. She consulted a handheld device for Sally-specific information, then rummaged through the plastic bag and examined Sally's medications systematically. Sally sat down in her easy chair. Maisie sat down across from her, lumped up, tense with unease. How foolish and stupid. What had she been thinking? After just a few minutes Sally nodded off to sleep. Maisie stood up. "I'll be back," she said without knowing when, exactly, or if saying so even mattered. Terry watched neutrally as she kissed Sally on the forehead and said good-bye.

BACK AT BEACH Haven a flock of gulls gathered noisily on the dune beside the house. A pair of joggers trotted past, middle-aged men in rhythmic business conversation. A note with a basket of cookies had been left at the front door by the landlord/agent. Enjoy! Maisie was eating them now, out on the deck with a cup of hot tea, a blanket across her lap. The sun was going down. It had been a mistake to leave Sally alone. All that crazy detail should have been a clue. Maisie should have been not amazed but alarmed.

She went inside and turned on the television. After five minutes she turned it off again. She ate the leftover chicken, showered, then got into bed feeling dropped from a great height, zoomed in, a squiggle. Was that what living in Alden's city would feel like? To nest in the crack of an enormous wall? A tiny squiggle. A chromosome. She lay on her side facing the open window. A breeze was blowing, and she could hear the ocean in the distance. Alden's aerial view of jungle ruins, his final moments. From ten thousand feet, five thousand feet. She could feel him plummet into the sprawling, centerless green canopy, into the absent core that now wound around and between them. His moment, now hers. She shuddered. It was enough. Yes, enough. And now the ocean silence was enough, more than enough, and a little emptiness a good, even maybe a beautiful thing.

She curled up, drew the covers tighter, wanting and not wanting to think about it. She was sad, very sad, but unable to cry. She had no photographs of Alden. Not a single one. There were photographs of her mother that Opa and Yva had kept and treasured. Baby, school. A family vacation in 1954, her mother as not one but two '50s American archetypes: lipsticked teenager and tourist in sunglasses. If there had been any photographs of Alden, they'd been excised, surgically removed. Yva and Opa had taken control and moved everything around like furniture for looks and comfort, putting this here, that there. She couldn't blame them. No photographs, no memory.

It was cold when she woke up. She went outside into the grey predawn. A heavy dew darkened the sand, formed a crust that her feet cracked through. The tide was out. She stood ankle deep in the chill surf, remembering now how she'd watched a sunset here with Sally all that time ago.

Right here. Perhaps she'd thought about that day from time to time over the years. Sure, she had. She must have. But she couldn't recall. It had had no weight before now, hadn't been etched or connected with anything before now. A line of birds flew by, skimming the surface of the water. A pungent seaweed smell. Water swirled around her ankles, drawing back out to sea in parallel channels. She felt the tiny, granular shift of yielding sand underneath her feet, mused about tides and currents and how long it would take to sink completely beneath the surface if she just remained standing there. In place.

Back at the house she emptied the box, looking for photographs. Now seemed the right moment to look. To open things up. She rummaged, eager and also dreading what might fall out, what she might discover. There were only a few; finding them was like being unblinded. One was of Alden walking on top of a pile of rocks. He looked worn and comfortable. She remembered his battered boots with the brass rings. His hair was shaggy, longer than she remembered, and he was wearing different glasses, not black horn-rims but tinted wire aviators. She studied the photograph. Who had taken it? And where? She dug around in the papers and found references to New Mexico, Arizona, Texas. There was a folder labeled Bogs—Denmark and another labeled Volcano—Stromboli but no indication that he'd ever been to either of those places. And, yes! There was a picture of Maisie. Eight-year-old Maisie proudly offering two eggs in her cupped hands with the tangled wire of Sally's chicken coop in the background. Had Alden taken it? She couldn't recall. But she did remember the clothes. She remembered them suddenly and vividly. Her favorite dress, corduroy, with a pocket bib, the blue-and-yellow striped tee shirt. She remembered the way it felt against her skin, and the eggs she'd gathered, and Sally's musty chicken coop with the shafts of light piercing through the holes and cracks. She also remembered Alden's camera and the way he looked holding the black box to his eye and the hollow little click when he pushed the button. It was so small against his face. Not a real camera but a toy pointing out at the future. It was all she could remember. She shuffled and sifted and tried to conjure, but there just wasn't any more. The shutter was drawn. Was that all that remained of the eight-year-old? What did Sally remember? And did it count? The old woman remembered reams and reams of stuff, spewed it out in an uninterruptedness of backward glancing, random reflection. To sink away like that, deeper and deeper into a phantasm. It was an illness, really. Maisie should have seen that.

Carefully Maisie packed up the box and gathered her things. She brought the deck furniture inside and emptied the fridge, then wrote a note to the landlord thanking him for the cookies and leaving her address for the security deposit. She closed and locked the windows and the sliding glass doors, drew the blinds. When she dropped the keys through the mail slot and heard the empty thud on the floor there was a split second of doubt. But there would be no going back. Maisie felt herself being lifted as she drove over the causeway, the sun breaking on the horizon behind her and salt air thrumming through the open windows at sixty mph. Up, up, up, over Manahawkin Bay and the flat expanses of empty marshland and overbuilt Beach Haven West with all its coves and landings. An image formed, an early morning. On Sally's front stoop with Alden. The sun had not yet come up, and the air was damp with a gauzy mist that hung in patches over the yard. A loud boom broke the silence. And then another and another.

"What's that?" Maisie asked.

"They're bombing," Alden said.

"Bombing?"

"Up at Warren Grove. A bombing range."

Another volley of explosions echoed. They listened as the booms rippled. Then a trio of fighter jets burst into view and shot upward in formation, three spiked arrowheads shearing straight up into the air, then, one by one, peeling away, leaving a bouquet of jet trails streaked across the sky. She ran out into the yard. Her heart was racing. Alden strode up beside her, shaking his head. She could feel herself rising from the ground with every bit the power of those jet engines. She wanted to tell him that she could fly, too. She wanted him to know that, if she wanted, she could extend her arms and shoot off, follow the dissolving trails of those supersonics into the empty landscape of the sky. Would he have thought her an angel? Divine and beautiful? Or just some odd creature with a gift she had no authority over and could not control? Vulnerable to falling.

"Hey! Look up there! It's Maisie! Hey, Maisie! Come down!"

She turned on the radio, flipped through the stations— and found Bruce Springsteen, of course. She sang along quietly, under her breath. Crazy Maisie and her mission man. "Crazy Maisie" she got called in high school, and sang with the sweet, belly-roiling recollection that only old pop songs can inspire.

She stopped for gas.

"Premium, right?" the attendant said with a knowing glance down the front of the car. She passed him her credit card, which he took between scissored fingers, dipped into the slot on the pump. He twisted off the gas cap, spun around, lifted the handle, and levered up the latch in the smoothest choreography of boredom. Maisie got out of the car to stretch her legs, watched the flowing traffic, the cars pulling into Taco Bell and Burger King and Nationwide Title Agency. The attendant washed her front and rear windshields, wiping the blade of the squeegee after each pull, thoughts entirely elsewhere, eyeing the traffic, the car pulling up at the adjacent pump. The tag on his shirt: Jerry. He skimmed back around, dropped the squeegee into a bucket, squeezed the pump handle once, twice, three times, looking back at the counter for just the right combination of numbers, then withdrew and replaced the pump handle, twisted the gas cap, and clapped the panel shut. A square little paper tongue slipped from the front of the machine. He tore it off with one hand, dipped the other into his shirt pocket for Maisie's credit card, which, completing his little ballet, he proffered again between scissored fingers along with the slivered receipt and an ever-so-slightly sardonic "Have a good one."

I will, she thought, pulling out of the parking lot. Yes. She was certain—and even had a picture of her certainty. Wasn't everyone certain pulling in and out of places? The crunch of tires—although tires didn't really crunch. It was a more subtle sound than that. But crunch and blue vapor were part of the picture. Part of the certainty. Sunlight flashed on the cars coming toward her, heading eastward toward the shore. She was a little point moving by indirection westward. Yes. She'd piece it all together. And all would fit, become part of the picture of moving forward, of turning the steering wheel with the aftward glance in the mirror and, glazed with certainty, being comfortably, calmly on her way.

Again she bought flowers at the Walmart—seven macrocephalous sunflowers.

"Oh, how big and colorful," the woman at the reception said when she walked through the automatic doors, cradling the nodding flowers in the crook of her arm. Maisie asked if she could speak with the director.

"Mr. Levinson isn't in yet."

"Can I make an appointment?"

"For today?"

The woman consulted her computer. "He has time at eleven."

The place seemed dank, the hallway narrower than yesterday. Rather than follow it all the way around to Sally's wing, Maisie went outside and followed the walkway that cut across the quad. An elderly couple sitting in the gazebo watched her from behind their trellised perch. Maisie waved to them as she passed. They followed her with their eyes.

She knocked softly, then rang. The door opened slightly, and Sally peered through the crack, smiled, and opened wide. "Sunflowers! My favorite!" She was in her slippers and nightgown, but her hair was neatly combed and pulled back, and her teeth were in place. Maisie offered the flowers, but Sally stepped back and bade her enter. Except for the unmade bed the room was unchanged from the day before.

"How do you feel today?"

"Oh, I'm okay."

The flowers from the other day were wilted in the big glass jar. Sally stood aside and watched as Maisie put them in the trash, rinsed and filled the jar with fresh water. "Do you have a knife or scissors?"

Sally thought for a moment, then pointed to a drawer by her bed.

"I'm sorry for what happened yesterday." Maisie took the scissors from the drawer, cut the stems to different lengths, and began arranging the flowers. Some had brown, some yellow coronas, and she arranged these browns and yellows again and again—and "There!" lifted and offered the jar.

Sally glanced at them. "Oysters'll drink whatever water you put 'em in," she said. "Fresh or salt. Clams are different."

"But these are sunflowers," Maisie said and set the jar on the table, not quite alarmed but with a sudden sinking feeling.

Sally went over to the balcony door and peered outside.

"We went to Green Bank yesterday, remember?"

"Green Bank?"

"We sat inside the church. I left you there and went for a walk down to the river."

Sally shifted over to her easy chair and sat down. Gingerly Maisie took the seat opposite, eyes fixed on Sally, who seemed both to be gathering herself together and also to be absorbed in something distant. There was a knock. The door opened, and a young woman put her head in. "Can I make your bed now?"

Sally brightened and waved. "Sure, honey. Come in."

"I'll just be a minute," the woman said and set straight to work.

Maisie stood up and went to the shelf with the carved decoys. The ducks were lined up on four shelves, facing in alternating directions. "They're all Ronnie's except one, am I right?"

"All Ronnie's except for three. And they're all valuable." She crossed the room, stood beside Maisie, and pointed. "The one on the end, the broadbill, that's a Rube Corliss. The black duck next to it is by Bill Cramer, and next to that, the merganser, Ronnie got from Ed Hazelton, who copied it from Rube Corliss. Rube taught Ed how to carve, and Ed taught Ronnie."

"Can I touch them?"

"Sure. Do you know how to hold a decoy?" she asked, leaning close and touching Maisie on the forearm. "Like you hold your girlfriend—by the breast and by the tail!" She laughed hoarsely. "A stupid carver joke. The men told 'em over and over a million times. Women had jokes, too. How do you make a bird carver quack? Grab his pecker!"

The woman making the bed laughed and plumped the pillow. Sally turned to her. "You know any good ones, honey?"

"Afraid not," the woman said, smoothed the blanket, and quietly left.

Maisie examined the ducks one by one, turning them over in her hands, feeling their remarkable balance, the smooth grain of the wood, the elegantly etched lines. "They've got lead in 'em for ballast," Sally explained, pointing to the opening on the bottom. "And none of 'em are waxed or have a shine. They were all meant for shooting over. Decorator ducks are waxed and shellacked. Won't attract ducks with a shiny decoy."

As Maisie studied each decoy again, Sally returned to her easy chair and described Ronnie's carving and how decoys and decoy carving had become a popular hobby. Originally, she said, hunters made their own decoys. "The meadows" used to be filled with thousands of lost, discarded decoys, and thousands more were burned for warmth. It was Fred Noyes, she said, who began the whole idea of collecting them. He was a successful businessman from someplace up in New England and came down to Lower Bank to die but ended up living there long enough to become the mayor. Eventually his collection got so big that he started a museum in Port Republic. "He had over five thousand carved decoys, all sorts of birds—geese, brant, black ducks, broadbills, canvasbacks, redheads. Wood ducks are scarce. So are pintails. Some of the best carvers in the whole country came from here," she went on, describing how Harry Shourds's father would sit down for a haircut and a shave and whittle a duck's head under the apron while the barber worked on him. "Left the barbershop with a smooth chin and a finished duck head every time!"

"Sally?"

"Yes, honey?"

"I'm sorry I left you yesterday."

"Left me?"

"In the church in Green Bank. Do you remember?"

Sally glanced toward the window. "Green Bank, you say?"

"Sally? Do you know who I am?"

The old woman didn't answer, kept looking toward the window. Then she turned to Maisie with an expression of blank helplessness and shrugged.

"I'm Maisie. Alden's daughter."

"Alden's daughter?"

Maisie squatted next to the chair and grasped Sally gently by the forearm. "You came to the beach with me. A house on the beach. We spent the night there, and yesterday we went to Green Bank."

"Alden had a little girl."

Maisie gave Sally's arm another squeeze and stood up.

"Cute little thing. Came to stay with me the summer of Alden's show."

"Show?"

"In New York. Some art gallery. What was it called? Doesn't matter. The show never hap—it never happened," Sally stuttered. "The girl burned his place down. The whole thing, burned right down to the ground. And all his work in it."

three

Maisie had had enough of being grounded. It was Christmas, and school was out, and the holiday lights were up all over the city. Her friend Veronica was with her mom, getting a snuggle muffle and hat at Franklin Simon and then going to Ohrbach's to look at the Coco Chanels in the Grey Room. It was supposed to snow. A big storm. Opa was eating breakfast and reading the paper, and Maisie could hear him complaining to Yva about Nixon and his men, who he said were all a bunch of gangsters. Maisie didn't want breakfast. She didn't even want to come out of her room. She was grounded for staying out too late with Mozart. Mozart was Mrs. Lasky's beagle. He'd run away, and it had taken her over an hour to find him. She'd flown up and down Riverside Park from Grant's Tomb to the Boat Basin, calling, "Here, Mozart! Here, Mozart!" for more than an hour. Some hippies who were sitting under a tree smoking pot heard her and started shouting, "Here, Beethoven! Here, Beethoven! Roll over, Beethoven!" They were all laughing and thought it was funny, but Maisie was scared of them and took off.

She'd been walking Mozart after school since the fall. It was her job. She always brought him to the park and tired him out playing with him. Even though she wasn't supposed to, she always let him off the leash and threw sticks and tennis balls for him until he got tired of fetching. He was over seventy in dog years and usually came when he was called. But he was also a beagle, and Mrs. Lasky said beagles were bred to follow their noses and would forget all their training in an instant to follow the trail of a scent no matter where it led. On her way home with Mozart, Maisie knew she was in big trouble when she saw Opa coming toward her all bundled up in his hat and gloves. He stopped short and did an exasperated little flap with his arms. She knew right away he was more irritated at having to come out in the cold than actually worried about her.

Mrs. Lasky was waiting up in the apartment with Yva. They were relieved the way grown-ups are when they aren't sure whether or not to be angry anymore. Maisie said she was sorry and explained that Mozart just suddenly took off and she couldn't catch him. "You had us very worried," Mrs. Lasky said. When she took out a dollar to pay Maisie Opa said, "No. Put it away." When Mrs. Lasky insisted he said, "No money," and put his hands in his pockets and looked down at the ground, which he only ever did when he was angry. Yva showed Mrs. Lasky to the door, and Opa gave Maisie the little nod that meant "I'll see you in your room."

He came in a few minutes later and stood there with his hands still in his pockets. "What you did was wrong," he said.

"But it wasn't my fault," she protested.

"You let him go. I know you did."

"But—"

"No buts. Mrs. Lasky told you never to let him off the line." His fuzzy grey look was also a look of grim satisfaction. Maisie was leaning against the windowsill on which were lined up her books, some stuffed animals, and the guppy bowl. Opa had a tank of guppies in his study with lights and coral and snails and seaweed and air filters that bubbled all day and night. Her guppies didn't have lights or an air pump, just colored pebbles and a plastic treasure chest. Her fish died sooner, but she could always take new ones from Opa's tank, which had an endless supply. He kept track of the generations. They were coming up on one hundred. Opa said that was more human generations than have existed for all of recorded history. Sixty-four generations takes us back to Roman times, and at eighty we are further back than Moses. Opa was very interested in generations and history. He pronounced it "chenerations." His accent made him sound unserious, and sometimes words came out of his mouth like something wet and chewy that he couldn't commit to swallowing. Yva always stopped him if he got talking about things she thought unsuitable for children, and Opa always obeyed her with a meek little nod. But when they were alone in his study, just the two of them, with the fish tank bubbling away in the background, he would smoke his pipe and talk freely and about everything. He also let her read his MAD magazines, which Yva didn't think was appropriate, either. They arrived every month in the mail. He kept them stacked in the corner behind his desk next to the radiator. He had a special chuckle when he was reading MAD. It wasn't laughter but more like practicing what it was like to laugh. He had an old friend named Kurt Magnus who liked MAD magazine, too. Professor Magnus had come to New York before the war, like Opa and Yva, and sometimes came to visit with his wife. Maisie could hear the men talking German and chuckling together through the closed door of the study. Mrs. Magnus and Yva sat in the living room and had tea and also spoke in German together but never chuckled.

Maisie was grounded not for letting Mozart off the leash but for lying. It was unfair. Maisie hadn't said anything about the leash, and Mrs. Lasky hadn't even asked. All she had said was that the dog got away. And that was true. But it didn't matter, according to Opa. When she asked him why the next day, he looked up as he lit his pipe—puff puff. "You want to know?"

Maisie nodded.

He took the pipe from his mouth and said, "The leash," which came out sounding like one word, zaleesh. He put the pipe back in his mouth, shifted it to the corner, puff puff. "It was brand-new." Maisie thought for a moment, not quite understanding. Opa watched her, puff puff. "Tell me. How did Mrs. Lasky's leash stay so nice and clean after for nearly an hour being dregged along the ground?" He flashed his twinkly smile. Puff puff. "Because it wasn't dregged. It was in your hand the whole time. Which can only mean you let him go." He took the pipe from his mouth. "And now you can go down to Mrs. Lasky and explain to her the whole story."

It wasn't fair. Especially since now it was Saturday, and she'd been down to Mrs. Lasky and said sorry, and Mrs. Lasky wasn't even mad. "I appreciate your honesty," she said and told Maisie she could still walk Mozart. "Just please keep him on the leash from now on."

Yet, still, she was grounded. And with no TV because of her report card, which she'd forgotten to bring home. It was in her desk. They could go by the school and get it anytime over the holiday. There weren't any F's on it. She'd just forgotten it in her desk, and that was the truth.

"What is the matter with you, Maisie?" Yva wanted to know. "Is something wrong?" No. There wasn't anything wrong. "Something you want to talk about?" No. They'd already talked about everything. There was nothing more. "You can ask us anything you like," they said. "You're old enough now." But Maisie couldn't think of anything to ask. Besides, Yva only talked about asking when Maisie was in trouble. It was her way of being mad without getting angry and scolding without losing her temper. She and Opa were old and had been through terrible things they never talked about. So why did they always ask her if she wanted to talk? Maybe they were trying to make up for the gap between their worlds. They were old-fashioned and different, and Maisie liked that they were different from regular American parents because it meant that she was different, too. She was glad Opa watched cartoons and read MAD magazine and called Nixon a gangster and liked guppies. She liked that Yva always dressed up to go out, even if it was just to Gristede's, and sometimes counted the money out loud when she paid for things. When Maisie asked why, she told her it was a habit left over from the inflation which, she explained, was a time when money was worthless. But why would you count money if it was worthless? Especially out loud! It didn't make any sense.

When she heard the phone ring Maisie ran to answer

it. Alden only called on Saturdays, usually in the morning around breakfast. Maisie couldn't call him because he didn't have a phone or even, really, a place to live. When he was in the city he stayed with a friend named Sol who was a sculptor and lived above a funeral home on 2nd Avenue just above Houston Street. It took up the entire floor. Alden only came into the city now and then. Mostly he was away, and whenever he called to say hi they'd talk until the operator interrupted and said to put more coins in the phone.

"Hi, Daddy" (she called him Daddy now, not Alden). "Where are you?" And he usually said, "Hey, Maze" (which was what he called her). "I'm in a partially buried shed in Ohio" or "walking along the shoreline of the Great Salt Lake" or "standing in a lightning field in the New Mexican desert." But this time he said, "I'm at Sol's. Want me to come get you?"

"I'm grounded."

"Grounded? That doesn't sound too good."

She felt a surge of relief. "Talk to Opa. Please. He'll let me go if you talk to him. It's so boring. Will you ask him? Please?"

"Are you in trouble?"

"Yes. But it wasn't my fault. Please. Will you talk to him?" When she looked up Opa was standing there. He held out his hand for the phone. He must have known already that Alden was in the city. She handed over the phone and retreated to the doorway to listen.

It was already afternoon when Alden finally came to get her. He looked different from the last time, with longer hair and tinted aviator glasses that he said were good in the desert, where he'd been living for the last half year. He had on Frye boots, all scuffed and cracked and worn down at the heels. Opa and Yva didn't pretend to be friendly. They didn't invite him in. Alden didn't seem to mind and gave them a little wooden box filled with rocks he said were from New Mexico. Yva's thank-you was stiff and cold, but Opa softened a little and accepted the gift, which Maisie later saw on the shelf in his study where he kept all the odd little trinkets he liked to collect—pebbles and shells and bits of colored glass and pieces of rusty metal he picked up here and there. Alden's box fit in perfectly. Maisie guessed it was because Alden knew what Opa liked. Somewhere deep down she knew they still cared about each other but couldn't show it because Alden was so irresponsible.

Duchamp looked different, too, with scrapes and scratches and rust on the bumpers. Inside, the cabinets rattled and the curtains were stained and tattered. They drove uptown to the Cloisters. On the way it started snowing. As they turned into Fort Tyron Alden rolled down his window and stuck his arm out for fun. Maisie copied him.

They drove into the park. The snow was sticking to the road and to the branches of the trees. There were just a few other cars, and it was suddenly quiet and felt like they were someplace far away. Finally they came to a parking area. "Did you watch the moon landing last summer?" Alden asked, rolling up his window. Maisie copied him and said she had. "Opa kept the TV on all day, and Yva cried."

"I cried, too!" Alden said.

Maisie thought he was kidding. "Why did you cry?"

"I don't really know." He turned off the engine and sat for a minute. "Some of the cowboys I was with were crying, too—though most of them were cheering and shouting. A whole wave swept through the place. It was wild."

"You were with cowboys?"

"At a bar in Reno. I'll never forget it. Did you cry?"

Maisie shook her head. She couldn't imagine him crying or being with cowboys, but she was glad he'd told her. He didn't usually tell her much about the places he went. Maybe it was because she was ten now and knew how to find them on a map. They got out and walked along a path in that quiet winter way that you can feel only with snow falling. There were old lampposts, some with broken glass, and crumbling stone walls with graffiti and worn-out benches to sit down on. She'd been to the Cloisters with Opa and Yva and on a school field trip. But not out in the park—which was gloomy and a little scary. With snow falling it felt like they were someplace far, far away. They came to the top of a hill. Alden looked down at Maisie's sneakers. "It might get slippery."

She showed him the bottoms of her sneakers, then followed him into the trees. There was no trail, but Alden seemed to know exactly where he was going. Their breath came out in big clouds. The ground was littered with cigarette butts and empty cans and broken glass. They came to a place overlooking the river. To the left was the George Washington Bridge. To the right the Cloisters rose up like a huge fairy-tale fortress, pinkish, splotchily wet with lots of windows and columns all huddled together behind big stone walls. The snow was just beginning to stick to the tiled roofs, which looked like fluttering white blankets with ruffled edges. A big barge was chugging upriver. Alden pointed to the cliffs of the Palisades across the river. "Over there. That's more or less what it looked like over here before Rockefeller built this place."

They sat down on a stone wall. Alden told her that the Cloisters had been built from the ruins of some medieval monasteries that had been torn apart stone by stone and shipped across the Atlantic. "To complete the illusion, Rockefeller bought up all the land over there to preserve the view. Imagine that!"

Maisie couldn't tell if he approved of it or not and took in the surroundings through the falling snow. Alden's hair was wet. He looked a little wild, and Maisie wondered what would happen if the police saw them there, if they'd run them off like they sometimes did to the hippies in Riverside Park. "It's not a monastery or church anymore but just something that has the flavor of those things all mixed and mashed up together," he said after a while. "But it's also more than a museum or a rich man's monument."

"What is it?"

"I don't know. Things always take on different meanings over time."

He talked for a while as if she were a grown-up—pointing and scratching things into the snow with the stick. She didn't understand much of what he was saying, but she listened closely. He asked her to think about how things change the places where they're put but also how places change the things that have been put there. "They're always connected. You can't have a place without putting something there. Even if it's something you don't actually set down but just a feature you notice. A rock formation, a tree. When you do that, notice or put something down, you've turned that place into something else. The thing you notice or put there is changed, too." He didn't stop to explain. It all sounded funny and strange. The snow swirled.

Her sneakers were soaked and her feet were cold, but she was happy to be there listening even though she had no idea what he was trying to tell her. Then he stood up and pointed to the fairy-tale fortress rising through the trees on the next hill and said, "Let's go look at the unicorn."

A short time later they were in a room hung with enormous tapestries. Alden pointed to a tapestry showing a unicorn surrounded by a wooden fence in a forest thick with plants and flowers. It was chained to a tree by a fancy collar and dripping with blood. "It's dead," Alden explained. "And in heaven. And so is everything in here, including the buildings." He pointed to the other tapestries hanging on the walls, to the fireplace with the carved stone mantel that reached to the ceiling, to the carved wooden doors and the stained-glass windows. "Everything in here was once part of a living world. But like the unicorn, it's all been killed and captured, removed to a perfect paradise to be kept and conserved forever."

They went out into the Cuxa Cloister and made a circuit around the little garden. Maisie followed Alden through the columned arcades, which he said were nearly one thousand years old and came from a monastery high in the Pyrenees mountains. He pointed out all the strange carvings: a man with a lion's body and a scorpion's tail, which he called a manticore; a woman with wings who lured men to their deaths with her beautiful voice, which he called a harpy. A griffon was a lion with wings and the beak of an eagle. Maisie already knew that a centaur was a man with a horse's body but not that the two-headed snake was called an amphisbaena. He led her into the Gothic Chapel. They looked at the stained-glass windows and the carved tombs of men and women with hands crossed and heads resting on tasseled cushions and feet propped on little dogs and lions. Maisie asked if the bodies of the dead people were still inside. Alden shook his head. "Can we see the unicorn again?" she asked.

They returned, and Alden shuffled again from tapestry to tapestry. His boots and wet, scraggly hair attracted the attention of the other visitors and a guard, who stood by the door with his hands folded over his belt, pretending not to be listening to what Alden was saying.

Finally they left and returned to the camper. "Are we going home?" she asked.

"No," Alden said. "There's something more I want to show you."

They drove down Broadway. The windows of the camper kept fogging up, and Alden gave Maisie a cloth and asked her to wipe the back window so he could see better. She climbed into the back and lay down on the crumbly foam padding. Even though the engine was right underneath and was noisy, it felt cozy to be back in the old camper again. She wiped the window with the cloth and watched while the city outside slipped by, sparkling wet and cold. They drove around for a while, and Alden finally found a parking space on 57th Street off 9th Avenue. Even in the snow shoppers crowded the sidewalks, and the smell of roasting chestnuts filled the air. Alden took Maisie's hand and said they didn't have time to stop because they were already late.

"Late for what?"

"For the opening."

"Opening of what?"

"You'll see." And he didn't say anything more.

When they were nearly at the corner of 5th Avenue he pointed up to a huge cross at the top of a building and said, "It's the French Legion of Honor. Like on a map. X marks the spot." He pointed out the frieze of golden sculptures above the second-floor windows and what he called caryatids high up at the top. It was hard to see in the falling snow. The buildings all the way down to the end of the block were dark and fenced and looked about to be demolished. When Maisie said the sculptures reminded her of the Cloisters, Alden smiled.

The gallery was called Dawn. It was brightly lit and painted completely white with bare floors. People stood around in little groups or milled around. Alden's work was laid out all over the room and took up most of the floor. He was standing behind Maisie with both hands planted on her shoulders, talking to a woman with a broad smile who was wearing a bright orange-and-yellow silk headscarf. She seemed to know Alden very well and kept bringing people over to introduce to him. They were looking at a group of lavender-colored metal boxes filled with sand, arranged in a hexagon and set on one of Alden's annotated topographical maps, blown up huge. The title, written on the wall behind it, was Non-place #1. The boxes were nicely shaped and arranged. The sand varied from box to box. Some was light, some coarse and dark. The map was familiar, too: light green background with orange and black lines, dark turquoise tufts for swampy lowland, and blue for streams and ponds. Suddenly she recognized it. "We rode bikes there!"

Alden smiled. Then he turned away as a man wearing a dark suit and tie stepped over and began talking. Maisie thought she understood now and was excited. There were suddenly lots of questions. Was the Cloisters like the sand in the metal boxes? All the stones and carvings and tombs had been brought from someplace else. Were the places they'd come from still the same places now without those stones and tombs? Putting things down and taking things away made a difference. But did it really matter? Was moving some sand from New Jersey into a building on West 57th Street the same thing as moving a tomb to a park at the top of Manhattan? Or a church or a monastery? Did bringing those old tombs to New York City take them away from France? Were they even tombs without the dead inside? If you dug up Grant's Tomb and set it down in Paris—or set a Parisian cemetery down in Queens—would they still be the same places? Maisie felt herself growing lighter and lighter. She looked proudly up at Alden, so handsome and cool with his messy hair and damp boots. She glanced around the crowded, brightly lit room, wishing she could lift off and float over them all, hover over Non-place #1 and become part of it like a real cloud floating over a real landscape. Clouds aren't part of a place the same way people are who view, move through it, and then vanish. The sounds in the room blended into a steady murmur. The light felt hot and began to pulse. Maisie's vision tunneled. She was lifted ever so slowly and began to float—up up up above the lights and conversations ringing all around—primary envelopment, authentic, animal faith reflections reflecting reflections, materials converging, plotting sculptural aspects of sedimentation—then, caught in a sudden downdraft, she let go.

VERONICA WAS TALKING about where her family always went skiing up in Vermont. She pretended it wasn't
bragging, but everybody knew it was. Maisie couldn't figure out why the other girls listened and even told Veronica how jealous they were of all the things she had and the
places she went. Maisie was glad the holidays were over.
She was happy to be back in school. What had she done
over the holiday? Where had she been? Even if she had
been in the mood to answer, what would she say? I was
grounded? I went to the Cloisters and then to look at my
dad's art work in a gallery? Even if she tried to make it
sound cool no one would understand. What was the point?
Better to just let Veronica talk about saunas and the chair-
lifts at Stowe and how funny her mother looked on skis
and how her father talked on the phone all morning and
one time got so worked up he forgot he was naked. So
embarrassing! The girls all chimed in with stories of their
holiday embarrassments. Should she tell them about losing
Mozart? That wasn't funny. There was also nothing funny
about Alden being told not to come back.

"We were just about to call the police" was the first
thing Opa said.

"Oh, verheavens!" Yva gasped and took Maisie by the
arm and tugged her inside. "Look at her! She's a mess!"

Alden apologized and began to explain, but Opa cut him off. "Completely inexcusable. We have been worried the whole day."

"Ve sought kitnapping—" Yva cut in, but Opa cut her off and said, "We talk in ze study."

Yva took Maisie into the bathroom and told her to strip off her wet clothes. She was groggy but not shivering anymore, like she had been when she woke up on the sofa with the gallery lady and Alden standing over her. The gallery lady gave Alden a wet cloth, which he pressed onto Maisie's forehead. Maisie squinted, feeling dizzy and light-headed. "You fainted," Alden said, holding her hand. The gallery lady brought a glass of water. The room was small and messy, with a desk covered with papers and walls covered with drawings and things that looked like they needed to be plugged in. Maisie could hear the show still in progress. Alden took the cloth from Maisie's forehead and helped her to sit up. He put the glass in her hand. "Sip slowly," he said and went over to the desk and picked up the telephone. He was calm and told Opa where they were. He said Maisie wasn't feeling well, and he was bringing her home. She could hear Opa's voice on the other end and knew that they were in trouble, though she wasn't sure what for. She ate a Baby Ruth bar going down in the elevator. The gallery lady said it would bring her blood sugar up and make her feel better. Alden tried to give her a piggyback on the way to Duchamp but had to put her down because the sidewalk was too slippery. When he suggested they stop for something to eat on the way, she told him she wasn't hungry, which wasn't true.

Listening to the other girls talk about all the embarrassing things that had happened over the holiday, she worried that what she had heard through the closed door of Opa's study was how things were going to be from now on. "No more coming and going as you please," Opa said. "You no longer have our trust." Some boys were playing with Zippo lighters over by the fence, flicking them open and rolling them down their legs to light them, waving them around like torches. A few were smoking cigarettes, holding the butts in their cupped hands and glancing furtively around. They were bragging, too; wanting to be seen and admired by the girls. But their bragging was different, and Maisie wondered what would happen if she just walked right over and demanded a cigarette and then slowly levitated and floated up to the roof and sat there with her legs dangling over the edge, tilting her head and blowing puffs of smoke casually into the breeze like the women in cigarette commercials. Not slinky Virginia Slims but Tareyton 100s, women who turned to the camera with a black eye and said, "I'd rather fight than switch." Two girls, Christine and Gina, had older brothers who had just been drafted to go to Vietnam. They were bragging, trying to prove who was more worried. Everybody was so powerless—Gina and Christine's brothers being sent off to Vietnam, Alden being told to stop coming over, which didn't seem right, either. Maisie supposed Gina and Christina were somehow proud of the danger of losing their brothers. But Maisie had nothing to be proud of in losing her father, and mostly she felt powerless.

Things got even worse when, a few days later, Opa went down to have a look at Alden's art exhibit and couldn't find any sign of it. Even the gallery had been closed. It was gone. If it hadn't been for a single advertisement in the Village Voice, where Opa had thought to look for verification, they would not have believed there had been any show at all. "Nothing but fly-by-night," was all Opa had to say, shaking his head. And though Alden had risen ever so slightly in their estimation for having had his name printed in the newspaper. Opa and Yva seemed to feel vindicated by the gallery's closing, as if the place and all the art in it had been brought down by mere association with her father. When, a day or two later, Alden called to say he was leaving, Maisie peppered him with questions. All he would say was that he was going on a long trip and promised to send postcards and call her when he got back. He was going down to Mexico, he said, and told her not to be angry with Opa and Yva. He said it was his fault and that when he returned they'd all sit down together and straighten things out. "For now the best place for you is right where you are. Your grandparents love you very much, Maisie, and so do I, and when you're older you'll understand and maybe forgive us."

When she told Opa and Yva, Opa said, "Mexico," only mildly surprised. He kept eating and didn't look at her. "Vell, I hope he has a very nice time," Yva offered primly. And Maisie realized not only that they already knew but that they were maybe even involved in his going somehow.

"Forgive," Alden had said. For what? For knowing something and not saying? Hadn't she been punished for that? Here was something much worse than letting Mozart off the leash. Everybody was pretending. Not saying, leaving things out. Was that what she would have to forgive when she was older?

Opa always sat at the head of the table, and in winter, when they ate Sunday dinner early, sunlight streamed through the windows in the living room. Usually he told her to draw the curtains if she hadn't already done it. This time, without saying anything, he got up and drew the curtains himself. Maisie was surprised. Watching the sun go down over the river was something she liked to do. Opa and Yva said it was one of the best reasons for staying on Riverside Drive. They had no plans to leave, even though they always complained that the city was so much more dirty and dangerous compared to when they'd arrived from Berlin in the summer of 1936, while the Olympics were still going on. Katherine must have done exactly the same thing, closed the curtains during Sunday at dinner. Her mother had grown up in the apartment, too, and died when Maisie was only three. When Opa got up to close the curtains Maisie knew they weren't telling her something and were hoping, like Alden, that one day she would forgive them. He came back to the table and resumed eating his meal as if he'd been opening and drawing the curtains himself all along—not asking that it be done for him. He was accustomed to being waited on. Yva, who waited on him, never complained but got even in a thousand mean-tempered little ways that were also like a kind of forgiveness.

It was as if a breeze had cleared Maisie's mind. Knowing there were things to be forgiven on all sides was like having the freedom to be as she pleased. And so the day Opa closed the curtains for himself, Maisie went from flying only over Riverside Park to flying over all of Manhattan and then over the entire metropolitan area. The best time for it was always before daybreak, when the city was quiet and the streets were practically deserted and everyone was still asleep. Bundled up against the cold, Maisie would swoop from her bedroom window and skim over the West Side Highway to the Hudson. If it was too cold over the river she'd fly over Morningside Park down to Central Park. She avoided the Reservoir and other open areas to keep from being seen. She'd stay just above the treetops, then zoom up quickly and fly over Midtown, where she was buffeted by gusts of air blowing up from huge ventilators on the tops of the buildings. She had to be very careful of downdrafts and crosscurrents. The spires of the Empire State and Chrysler Buildings were always tempting, but she kept her distance from them. The Pan Am Building was also dangerous because of the helicopters that sometimes took off and landed there. It was Opa's favorite new building. He liked to mention that he'd met the architect, Walter Gropius, in Berlin before the war. As soon as she passed the great glass slab she'd go higher and head toward the two towers rising up by the Battery. They were nearly finished and looked like big steel thermometers, with the silver mercury rising to a different level on each one and little spidery cranes perched on top. Then she'd either bank hard and climb high over the West Side piers that jutted into the Hudson River like the teeth of a comb or turn the other way and fly out over Governors Island toward the Outer Bay, weaving among the harbor gulls and looping back around the Statue of Liberty and Ellis Island. Or she'd fly up the East River, over

Fulton Market to the Brooklyn Bridge, then cut back into Manhattan to fly around some of the older buildings. She preferred the older architecture because there were decorations and crags and crannies to nestle and hide in. The Barclay-Vesey was her favorite because it had bulk and lots of setbacks and battlements and wasn't too fussily ornamented, like the Woolworth building, which was heaven to fly around but horrible to land on. She had scrapes and bruises from bumping into gargoyles and slipping from crazy tracery and sills and ledges that were always a little steeper and narrower than they looked. There was also the problem of pigeons and their droppings, which was why Maisie's flying gear was so dirty. She had to keep it hidden in the back of her closet. Her gloves were especially filthy, a fancy old leather pair of Yva's that came up to her elbows.

It wasn't long before she outgrew filthy clothes and Yva's gloves and zooming and scrambling around like a little bee buzzing from flower to flower. So she learned to fly higher and farther—more like a bird, not a bug; with a point of view, not just a position. She didn't need to be going anyplace. Just being up there was enough, in level flight or climbing, soaring, diving. What made her feel sorry for ordinary people was not that they couldn't do it but that they didn't know such a thing was even possible. If Maisie did ever reveal her gift to the world, which temptation she vowed to resist to the end of her days, describing the perfect joy that flying gave her would be impossible—except to say that it was something like forgiveness, which can't be forced or measured and must also simply happen, and that life without it is incomprehensible.

She could see a good distance up and down the Hudson from her bedroom window. If bad weather made it impossible to go out, just sitting at the window was enough to relieve the loneliness that came from doing nothing. It wasn't that she was bored. But the days had a way of running together into a soupy sameness. Flying was all she had, and she didn't need fantasies to explain how she did it. Wild nature was enough, being just a tiny speck, no different from a sparrow or a moth or a particle of floating dust.

Over the years the apartment grew mustier and thicker with its oriental carpets and shelves filled with books and things Opa and Yva had acquired over the long years. The leather sofa was cracked and soft; the coffee table in the living room was stained and piled with books; the crystal centerpiece on the dining table contained dried flowers and nuts that nobody ever ate. The guppies in the study were long gone. When Opa lost track of the generations he also lost interest in keeping them. Maisie talked him into getting a parrot, a scarlet macaw he named Vico—after the philosopher Giambattista Vico, whom he was for a time writing a book about. A plaque attached to the cage read Verum esse ipsum factum, which Opa said meant "The true itself is made." But for the bird's eruptions, the apartment was quiet. Vico would squawk and drag his beak across the bars of the cage. Maisie would give him bits of apple or cucumber. He was a beautiful bird with yellow and blue wing patches, a red head and tail. He would take the cucumber in his beak, then drop it and do his mocking little neck dance and scoot over to the far end of his perch.

If macaws were among the longest-lived creatures on the planet, spiders were among the shortest-, and Maisie liked them, too. For a while there was a big cobweb in the corner of her bedroom. She watched it grow for some time, a dense, milky structure, well anchored. She'd once read a book that described a man (but shouldn't it have been a woman?) building a web between Saint Paul's Cathedral and Ludgate Hill in London, scrambling across rooftops and between chimneys, climbing over shop fronts and awnings, rushing down crowded streets, uncoiling and paying out rope, dodging traffic, frenetically climbing and joining and fastening, and then, at the end of a long day's work, settling into a little apartment and installing a telephone line to be informed when visitors arrived—so that he could eat them. It wasn't the dark intention or the heroic effort of web building that Maisie admired; it was the image of a thread shot from the belly rising up, up, up on the wind, a delicate, strong thread wafted and carried aloft. That was beautiful.

And what about her? Was she, Maisie, beautiful? She pretended not to care. But the truth was, she did. Alone in her room, she cared. Walking down the street, she cared, though she always pretended she wasn't looking at her reflection as she passed some plate-glass surface or walked by a mirror. There were other vanities, too. Emotional ones. Keeping them in check was much harder work. Sharps and flats and edges. Weariness. Underwhelm-ment. She would put her feet on the coffee table and sit with a book in her lap, Vilhjalmur Stefansson's account of his third arctic expedition. She loved reading about arctic exploration, about Eskimos and polar bears and whales, about picking fish out of nets at forty degrees below zero, water boots made of sealskin, wrecked schooners, perpetual daylight, perpetual night. She loved reading in low-wattage comfort on the sofa, the ocher-and-indigo Persian carpet on the floor.

When she couldn't concentrate she held the book in her lap and stared into the empty familiarity of the living room. Then she would look at the book, stare down into it. Her eyes tracked the sentences, but the words merely joined together and were gone. When we went to sleep the camp became exceedingly cold … an Indian gets lost as easily as anybody …

She wanted to be empty and clear—not buzzing, disconnected, synchronized like the rhythmic patter of footsteps. Was she ordering the sound? Or was there rhythm everywhere, a dancing, shuffling precision suffusing the cosmos that one vibrated to like a rolling train, clickety-clack clickety-clack?

Vico squawked.

She put aside the book, grateful for an excuse. Some demon was sneering at her from inside, making her think a purposeful, higher order was being neglected, time was being frittered and wasted, time that was valuable, precious, and eluding her. Stefansson's description of the winter spent at Tuktuyyaktok with an Eskimo family. The lamps were kept lit with slabs of polar bear or seal fat, which slowly dripped over the flame into a bowl containing the wick. Ingenious. She wasn't keeping up. With what? A slab of fat suspended on a hook over a flame? A spiderweb? Why did her thoughts wander? Why couldn't she snuff them?

Vico had tucked himself off to bird sleep. Maisie's toes needed a touch-up. Maybe a new red. She had nice toes. "Great toes," according to Veronica. She didn't color her fingers. Just toes, which she flexed into a row of little chairs with red cushions. She picked up the phone to call Veronica.

"We're going to Costa Rica day after tomorrow. The rain forest."

Maisie listened. In general she only listened. Veronica was the talker, she the listener. Being on the phone usually made her sleepy. It wasn't boredom. She loved Veronica. They'd been friends forever. Even if all Veronica did was talk about herself. She liked that they were completely different. Funny. Veronica was talking about her younger brother. "It's something at school, I'm pretty sure. The drama. Stomachache. Headache. Yesterday he wouldn't get out of bed, said he had chills. He must've touched the thermometer to a lightbulb or dunked it in hot water or something. 'Good lord! You've got a one ten!' 'We need an ambulance. A hundred and ten.' You should've seen his face!"

Veronica's laugh came through the phone like a clutch of escaped balloons. Maisie laughed, too. It warmed her. They said their good-byes. She put the phone down, covered Vico's cage for the night. The telephone rang. Veronica calling back? Would it wake Opa and Yva? She didn't feel like talking anymore. The answering machine in Opa's office clicked on. She listened to the message being left, some colleague from the university, then the cradle clunk, the long beep and the whirring rewind of the cassette. Then silence. It was the silence that reminded her—and the little red light on the top of the machine that blinked afterward to show a message had been left. She couldn't help it. When she thought of Alden now it was purely speculative, a sensation she had no word for. A non-feeling. She went on, doing everything as always. School. Friends. Books. Music. Movies. TV. She grew up. Opa and Yva got old. Instead of Sunday dinner they started going down to Chinatown for dim sum, Jing Fong Restaurant on Elizabeth Street. Yva loved brunch and not having to cook. Opa loved Chinatown and dim sum. It made him happy to show how, if one left the lid open, a new pot of tea would appear like magic out of the clamor and chaos. His uncle Max had gone to Shanghai and died there before the war. Opa knew so much about the world. And Yva, who'd learned to relax her old world manners, pointed and chose from the steaming, dish-laden carts, delighted. Maisie was most fully their daughter in those moments of being taken to big, crowded places and shown tiny things. But to feel something missing? She couldn't. There was nothing to remember. Her days and years had long been squashed and flattened out. Time had taken care of that, buried the details in the vast white snowfield with only gentle undulations of the landscape to mark the humps and hummocks of what had been: the friends she'd had and what they had done together; the places she'd been; a college year in Avignon, classes and beaches and trains and buses, back home to the tarry street smells and the rattle and drip of window units in summer, the sparkle of light off the river and the Gulf Western Building on Columbus Circle and people packed into the Sheep Meadow for Simon and Garfunkel and the Talking Heads and crammed in at the Mud Club and CBGB. Whom had she gone with and whom had she met? What had she done? Where had it gone? Did you simply follow the links, hand over hand, not caring where you began, which direction you drew in—forward? backward?—but simply drew, hand over hand, link to link, and-then-and-then-and-then, until all evaporated and left you, quieted, nowhere? Or was it not chains and links but more like a large flock of starlings abruptly and suddenly changing direction all at once? A graceful brushstroke across the sky. Spontaneous, unprovoked.

"WHO IS IT?"

"Maisie, your niece. We spent last week at the shore together, remember?"

"Maisie, honey!" Sally crooned, as if they'd only just parted ways.

"I'm sorry I had to leave so suddenly."

"We had a wonderful time, didn't we? A real vacation."

"And thank you for the box, Sally. I've been going through it slowly. There's a lot in there to think about."

"Alden's box?" Sally's voice clicked into another register, and she veered into talking about an elm tree struck by lightning and collecting laurel for Christmas wreaths. Maisie wondered if there was someone in the room with her. "Sally?"

"Yes, honey?"

"Are you still there?"

"Me? Yes. I'm here."

Then she wasn't.

Maisie put down the phone. Besides the building, there had been nothing to see. A Bolton's and a bunch of dentist's offices. Still, she was glad she'd gone to look, thinking it was what Sally would have done. She had stood on the south side of West 57th Street, scrolling around on her smart phone to discover what she could of number 29, the ornate Beaux-Arts building that had once been called Chickering Hall. Standing on the sidewalk, she read about the École des Beaux-Arts in Paris, the French Legion of Honor, the history of piano manufacturer Chickering & Sons and piano halls and Oscar Wilde. She remembered Alden pointing to the cross at the top. A big, beautiful cross marking the spot.

But now it was mirrored in the concave glass slope of the building next door, already decorated for Christmas with enormous candy canes. Had that been there? The Avon Building? She couldn't recall and checked the dates. No. It hadn't. She took some photographs, crossed the street, took some more. Then she put her phone away and went home. It was enough. She'd had enough. If there was satisfaction in returning to the place, there was dignity in letting go and forgetting, in being gone and forgotten. Forgiveness, too.

She turned on the television to break the silence. The BMW Masters tournament was being played in Shanghai. She watched indifferently, cutting eyes to the television. She was blank, could conjure nothing more from her memory than faded outlines, like the view from the living room window now as a child rode by on a bicycle, a thereness she simply observed from a distance.

"Do you love him?" Sally had asked.

"Who?"

"Who? Your husband, honey. Or is there someone else?"

It caught her off guard. Rather than answer she just shook her head.

"It's all right, honey. I never knew the answer to that one, either. Just trying to remember what it was like, that's all. It's a lot less personal than you think."

"What what was like?"

"When I realized that loving someone isn't at all what I thought it was and maybe isn't anything more than—" And she broke off and smiled, turning her palms up in her lap.

"More than what?"

"Paying attention," she said and laughed. "Only good thing about getting old is you have more time to do it."

Maisie smiled, only now realizing that Sally had not been offering elderly wisdom but pulling something sad from the scattered snowdrifts of her attentions. Paying attention while no longer the object of anyone else's.

A short time later Maisie was in the car. It was cold out, the November sky a canopy of sheet-metal grey. The ribbon of highway signage tunneled and flashed in a blur of regular shapes and colors. It was absurd to be out driving aimlessly, but it also felt necessary, natural. To be moving and yet so still in the rolled-up quiet of the car, going no place. She had nothing to complain about, nothing to regret. There were things she couldn't remember and things that had faded that she must keep and live with as they now were, stop joining what couldn't be rejoined and disjoining what had taken all these years to be joined. Where did her fits of dissatisfaction come from? These downdrafts that made it impossible to get off the ground?

When she called back Sally was completely lucid. Maisie

pulled into a Pizza Hut parking lot and came straight out with it. "Would you want to come and live with me, Sally?"

"That's awfully nice, honey. But I don't know. Can I bring my ducks?"

"Of course."

"You're in the car, you say?"

"Yes."

"Are you coming by?"

"No. Just driving around. How are you feeling today?"

"Where'd you say you are?"

"Montclair, driving toward Paterson." There was a stutter in the connection. "What was that? I couldn't hear you."

"Whoopee Road."

"Whoopee Road?"

"Where you go for whoopee." The laugh. "Whoopee Road ran right through Pestletown."

"Paterson, not Pestletown." Maisie laughed. She listened as Sally rambled on about the state licensing certificate hanging in the doctor's office (it was a nice pink color), the king-sized steaks at the old Berkeley-Carteret Hotel in Asbury Park (you got a room and all meals), and the Beach Comber News (going out of business) and came back again to Whoopee Road and Pestletown. Then lost track and went silent.

"Sally?"

"Yes, honey?"

"I'll call back tomorrow. Okay?"

There was no reply.

Maisie hung up, noting as she depressed the button on the steering wheel how much more severe the ensuing silence was than the good-bye clunk of cradled handsets and how clunky it made her feel to remember such a thing, and drawn closer to her limits. She continued driving, feeling swallowed up by the car, the road. How had she ended up here? What had she been doing for twenty-six years? Don had talked her into suburbia. She'd been charmed at first, drawn in by his friendly and tightly knit family, by the big trees and old houses. They bought one of them, a rambling, tree-shaded Dutch Colonial with a detached garage that they'd turned into a pottery studio. Part of what had persuaded her to leave the city was Don's complete indifference to her city preferences. "Does a three-bedroom on Riverside Drive really make a fuller, richer life?" She'd sold the apartment, inherited when Yva died in 1988, just four years after Opa. To keep it had felt all wrong. She was glad to sell and happy with what she got. It irritated her when people talked ruefully and with odd vanity about the places they'd let go. She felt a curious mix of estrangement and belonging whenever she drove down the West Side Highway.

Sally's oscillations from in-the-moment lucidity to disconnection and retreat were more frequent and severe than Maisie had at first realized. What bothered her was not that they signaled mental deterioration and a worsening condition but that they formed a perfect reverse image of her own amnesia, a disconnection and retreat from her past. Living in the rambling moment felt unballasted. And the present was not all a grand, moving pageant but a hard current Maisie struggled rudderless against. Was the one any more connected to anything than the other? Maisie had always been seen—mostly because she was a potter and mostly by Don's family—as mellow, pragmatic, centered. The very opposite of an unhappy woman. It made no sense to her. Being stuck in the rambling present was as tedious as being lost in a vaporous past—and just as hard to endure.

The traffic slowed. Holiday decorations were strung along the facades of box stores and draped across parking lots and lampposts, a confetti of electric lights. She turned off the GPS. What was she asking for but to know which way to go, how to get places?

Being lost was scary—and the only way to not be lost was to know, always, where certain places were and how to get to them. But that also meant knowing always where you were in relation to those places—and what if you didn't or they were gone, had vanished? To know how to get home was one thing. But maybe it wasn't enough.

Maisie wanted Sally to come live with her because Sally was her only living relative, her aunt. And old and frail and lonely. It seemed a good way to make up for so many things. But was she overlooking something? If so, what could it be? She didn't know. It didn't matter. That she was able to. That was good enough.

She returned home sometime later, after a stop for groceries. The television was still on, and the sound of the golf announcers cut through the silence of the house. The respectful hush in their voices contributed to the mystique of a game whose entire appeal was a mystery and why she liked to watch it. Golf was played in calm yet ended in euphoria and yielded nothing. It was just the antidote to the backward pressure that bringing Alden's box into the house had started.

She was still not sure what it added up to. The legacy of a real artist or just abandoned ephemera? Out of the box it all had come, piece by piece, bit by bit. She was meticulous about conserving the order and made notes as if excavating an archaeological site. Envelopes and file folders were carefully opened, their contents numbered with a soft lead pencil. There were four large wooden cigar boxes filled with knickknacks of the sort Opa might have accumulated, six mason jars containing different types of sand, black-and-white photographs, 35-mm color slides, reels of 8-mm film in metal cans, matchbooks and printed napkins and index cards held together by crumbling rubber bands, and pages and pages of writings, notes, and maps. An astonishing volume of material exploded from the box over the course of several days, expanded and spread across the room into little galaxies and constellations. It all seemed perfectly formed.

YOU GREW UP in South Jersey?

Yes.

In the Pine Barrens?

Yes. I'm a Piney. We didn't always like being called that. Not by outsiders, anyway.

Did you come from a big family?

No and yes. I was an only child. When I was thirteen my parents were killed in a car accident, and I went to live with my uncle. It was kind of an extended-family situation.

So you stayed in the area and went to school there?

Yes. For a while. When I was sixteen I got a scholarship to the Art Students League and went to live in New York.

How did you manage that?

An old friend of my parents', a painter named Ned Knox. He suggested I apply. I made some prints and sent them, and they accepted me.

What kind of prints?

Woodcuts. I guess you'd call them Expressionist landscapes. I used to go out in the woods to paint with Mr. Knox. He told me not to draw or paint the way he did. I thought at first he didn't want me copying him. When I was fifteen he took me to the Philadelphia Museum of Art, and I realized he meant something very different.

Very different than not copying him?

Yes.

Different how?

Different in every way that could be imagined. When I got to New York I saw there was something going on that had everything and nothing to do with what I thought painting was.

When was that?

August 1955. I stayed with an old friend of Ned's. Milton Passlof. Abstract Expressionist wasn't a household word yet. But he was one of them. A member of the Club that met on 8th Street. He lived on 8th Street. Number 47. The neighborhood was all painters and studios. Galleries opening up. They weren't called galleries. They were called co-ops. Milton had been in the war. I think I was as impressed by that as by anything else. He treated me like an adult right from the start. He liked to argue and talk and hated the Art Students League. Just hated it. Now he's giving talks there, by the way! Anyway, I was tolerated.

How long were you at the ASL?

Not long. I left after a few months. School, classes, didn't do much for me. And I had all these bad influences! I took life drawing for a while with an old WPA friend of Milton's, Issac Soyer. He had a studio up near Central Park and was a communist. I was too young to understand most of what was happening around me. But I could see exciting things were going on. I got a job delivering telegrams, Western Union, and just made myself very small and watched and listened. There was always lots of talking and arguing—even fights. Everyone knew what everyone else was doing and who was getting famous. Lots of jealousy and meanness.

It must have been very exciting.

Yes. But mostly it scared me. I'd lie on my mattress behind the wooden milk crates stacked up in a far end of Milton's loft. It was a big space. Everything was big. The paintings, the spaces. Just huge. And I was a little dwarf peeking out at all these bigger, older people—plenty of them were just crazy, out of their minds. Gradually I began to understand what was going on. And that it could be done only once, that it was being done now and would be forever done with afterward. Things were being drawn to some kind of conclusion. Milton always said he was exhausted. I'd watch him put paint onto these huge canvases for days and weeks. Paint is heavy! Those canvases weighed a ton! And the more paint he slapped on the more frustrated he'd get. "What am I doing?" he'd always ask. All spattered. "What is this crazy thing I'm doing? This monster. How do you paint a picture without all these things that make a picture?"

So you started painting, too?

No. I joined the army.

You were in the army?

Not for long. I went to basic training. Got sent to Fort Knox—which I always thought was funny because of Ned. I was discharged after less than a year. They didn't have much use for me. I was a lousy typist. I came back to New York for a while. To Milton's. He was pleased that I'd gone off and happy that I came back again. He was very generous and good to me. Treated me like a son. Anyway, that's when I began to paint.

At Milton's?

No. I went back to South Jersey. My uncle had an old cabin on his land that I turned into a studio.

How did you support yourself?

There was always construction and odd work to be had. I liked being outside, working on road crews. The New Jersey Turnpike was being extended. I'd work for a week or two, then go off to my shack and paint.

Did you show any of that work?

No. It's gone.

Gone where?

It doesn't exist anymore. It was burned.

You destroyed it?

It was destroyed. Yes. Which freed me to do what I've been doing ever since.

Your non-places?

Yes.

THAT WAS ALL. It was incomplete. Two printed pages torn from a gallery brochure slipped in among some photographs of a construction site and a list of anchor-lock radius forms from the Gates & Sons Concrete Forms Company in Denver.

Maisie's hands trembled as she slipped it back into place, as if returning it to a hiding place she'd inadvertently stumbled upon. When, a few minutes later, she opened the notebook for another look it was just to inventory the other items, what it had lain among for all this time. If there were clues, she didn't want to lose them, and if there weren't, there was magic enough in the dispersion of items, things that Alden had placed there for whatever reason—only to be chanced upon by her these many decades later.

On the coffee table were two prints. One was titled A Bird's-Eye View of Egg Harbor City with a label that read, in Alden's hand, No summer (lost) is so summery as the memory of summer. The map showed the town grid, buildings and people and horse-drawn carriages. A little steam engine billowing smoke chugged by in the foreground. Maisie recalled Sally telling her that a railroad line was supposed to connect the city to the river but was never built. A harbor city without a harbor, she'd called it.

The second, dated 1924, was an "Aero View" and bore an insignia that, insisting a little too much, read, "Egg Harbor City. A Place of Industry, Health, and Happiness. The Ideal Spot for Your Home. All Roads Lead Here." Maisie wasn't sure whether either map showed a real place or a fantasy. Maybe they were simply projections of a projection. In the upper left of the earlier view the Mullica flowed from the sharp bend at Sweetwater all the way down to Green and Lower Bank, where, with amazing detail, tall ships were depicted coming and going. It was a view that, in 1864, could only have been that of a bird—not strange and distant but miniature, charming, and somehow cozy. It drew her in, made her want to zoom from detail to detail, soar above the lively animation to a purely interior place she could step back from with a date and a horizon and an invisible, wholly private place in her heart. The Aero View, by contrast, contained no human figures. It situated itself proudly in miles distant from Baltimore (100 mi), Philadelphia (40 mi), Trenton (50 mi) , New York (90 mi), Great Bay (13 mi), Atlantic City (18 mi), Ocean City (18 mi), and Cape May (46 mi). But, for all its grand certainty, it was less a place than a site of annihilation.

At the very bottom of the box she'd found a large manila envelope containing a green leather- and clothbound folio of prints titled Views of Ancient Monuments in Central America, Chiapas, and Yucatán by F. Catherwood, published in London in 1844. It looked valuable. She spent an entire day going through the maps and colored lithographs of crumbling but still inhabited monuments overtaken by dense Central American jungle. It occurred to her that Alden's city must have been inspired by them. Perhaps they had also been his reason for going to Guatemala. The romanticized depictions emphasized the sites as ruins and showed the Mayan inhabitants merely as local fauna, completely indifferent to the monuments among which they lived. Alden's city was to be a living ruin set down in a place where history had been effaced entirely. It was a return to wilderness dictated by a civilization that had obliterated it everywhere else.

Maisie had been two hours throwing pots. But for the sound of the turning wheel, the studio was silent. It was after midnight. She leaned forward and peered down into

the cylinder rising on the wheel, then withdrew her hands, blew a dangling strand of hair from her face, and slowed the spinning wheel until it came to a stop. Tired from hunching over, she stood up and stretched, gently rotating her head to ease the tension in her neck, twice clockwise, twice counterclockwise. The wet bits of sponge she'd used to smooth the rim looked like pumice ejected from a volcano. She liked to think of what she did with her hands in geological terms. As elemental, physical labor, throwing a lump of clay onto the wheel and turning out a form. And doing it again and again and again. What made it possible year in and out was this: she never hurried. She let the forms take shape, each one in its turn, and moved on to the next. If there was no urgency in the rest of creation, why hurry making a pot? She started the wheel again. With one hand inside the revolving cylinder, she gently lifted the clay walls higher and higher and saw her own self forming in the process, bit by bit, pot by pot, assuming her place in this unhurried way out of an inborn urge she didn't fully understand but knew her life would be meaningless without.

There was no moon. She took a deep breath, rose up through the sketch work of tree branches overhanging the studio and into the radiant orange glow of starless, metropolitan night. She didn't hurry. It took a few minutes to become oriented. At a thousand feet the entire metropolitan region was visible, a vast, glittering carpet. Looking north, she could see the black strip of the Hudson where it curved gently westward above the Tappan Zee. To the east a good portion of Long Island stretched broad and flat between the Sound and the Atlantic Ocean. Continuing south took her over Bayonne and the two enormous port terminals jutting into Upper New York Bay at the mouth of the Kill Van Kull. They looked to Maisie like ghostly imprints of the vanished World Trade Center towers. Following this bearing, she went over the Verrazano Bridge and grazed the tip of Staten Island, where to the left she could see Coney Island and the tip of Breezy Point and the Rockaways. Across Lower New York Bay was the dangling appendix of Sandy Hook and the gigantic trident of Naval Weapons Station Earle, which extended three long, slender miles into the bay. She passed between Fair Haven and Red Bank and over the Navesink and Shrewsbury Rivers just west of Asbury Park, Neptune City, Avalon, and Belmar. She flew directly over Point Pleasant until she finally reached the water's edge over Seaside Heights. She adjusted her bearing by a few degrees to avoid flying out over open ocean, then adjusted it again slightly over Barnegat Light, from where she had a clear view over Surf City and Ship Bottom down to Little Egg Inlet at the tip of Long Beach Island, where the Mullica empties into the Great Bay.

Thinking of Sally, she banked at Little Egg Inlet and flew up the Mullica, then turned into the empty barrens over Alden's city midway between the Green Bank and Lower Bank bridges. She dropped down to just over a thousand feet and circled the area once, then turned due north and flew over the dark forest and the miles and miles of dirt road that ran through it in long, straight lines leading nowhere. On the horizon to her right she could see the slight fire tower–topped elevation called Apple Pie Hill.

Following some instinctual inertial guidance, she banked and began a gentle corkscrewing descent until she

was no more than one hundred feet above the treetops—
the planned height of Alden's Jetport terminal.

Then she slowed, scanning from east to west to locate
the place where, according to Alden's drawings, an enormous slab would thrust out from the canopy at a low angle,
a soaring monument marking the interpenetrating bound-
ary of air and land, a supersonic jetport cut into the forest, a
shard of tectonic plate erupted from deep inside the earth's
interior like exposed broken bone. Skimming along the top
of the forest canopy, she wondered if it was a wound he
wanted to inflict or if it meant something else entirely.

Maisie zigzagged, heading toward the center of the vast emptiness curtained on three hundred sixty degrees of the horizon by starlight. It was cold and her joints began to ache and she was tired. At night she liked being closer to the ground. Even over an empty forest, the scale was more comforting. In daylight she flew at higher altitudes, where the dendritic geometries of flowing rivers and the contours of fields and ridges left by long-vanished ice sheets shifted the view onto a geologic scale and she was no longer looking down at a landscape but at the Earth. It was rarefied, cold, and frightening. She preferred the lower altitudes, where she could breathe more easily and see the ground at the scale of human contact where land and scape cohered.

At night the moon was her main point of reference, but her way was also lit by the patterned network of roads and highways below. The Garden State Parkway, the New Jersey Turnpike—which soon came into view on the horizon. She knew every glittering mile of that highway and could tell her exact position with lazy certainty by simply looking down. She now saw clearly why Alden's city had to have that chromosomal look: to show that the linkages that connected the people living there with each other also connected them to the place, to all its natural features. It was a vision of both intimacy and vastness—without being picturesque in any way. She climbed to a thousand feet and followed the turnpike north to the Garden State, where she increased her altitude again and followed the meandering unloveliness of northern New Jersey's sprawling patchwork to the Eagle Rock Reservation. She descended quickly and with a hop and a skip over Bloomfield and Claremont Avenues dropped silently, pulse racing, into her own backyard.

"YOU WANT TO give away my room?"

"Not 'give away,' Karl. Move."

"What about my stuff?"

"We'll find places for everything, honey. Don't worry."

"Who is she again?"

"My aunt Sally."

"You never said you had an aunt, Mom."

"She's not an aunt, actually. More of a cousin, I think."

"Well, you never said you had any cousins, either. Who is she?"

"My father's cousin Sally. I spent a summer with her when I was little but lost touch after my father died."

"How did you find her?"

"I didn't. She found me. It's a long story, honey. I'll explain when you get home. When is that, by the way?"

"Exams are over the week before Christmas."

"Have you made plans with your dad?"

"We're going skiing after Christmas."

"Where?"

"Stowe. One of the partners has a house there."

"Have you booked your flight?"

"I'm driving with Dave, my roommate. He has a car. Will she be moved in already?"

"I don't know. She may not even agree to come. I wanted to make sure it was okay with you first."

"You said she's senile?"

"She has dementia. But it kind of comes and goes. You'll like her. I wouldn't be doing this if I had any doubts about that."

"What's she like?"

"It's hard to say. She's kind of a throwback in a down-home kind of way. You'll see."

"Did she know Opa and Yva?"

"They didn't acknowledge my father or his family. I think I've told you that."

"Mom?"

"Yes, honey?"

"Are you going to be okay?"

ALL ALONE IN the house, sitting on the floor of the den with the contents of the box strewn over the room. She put away the manuscript she'd been reading—fifteen typed pages of crinkly onionskin titled The Dizzy Syntaxes of Infra-Criticism. It made only the dimmest sense to Maisie. She puzzled through the sentences as if deciphering a long-lost letter and talking to herself at the same time. She pulled out a yellowed index card on which Alden had written a quotation: Nature is an infinite sphere whose center is everywhere and whose circumference is nowhere. On the reverse side was written Or: whose circumference is everywhere and whose center is nowhere.

She felt something pulling at her, not something big and rooted drawing her down but something thin and tenuous, a wafting thread. It wasn't something she was missing or pined for. So much was gone, forgotten, didn't matter. She could feel herself detaching, leaving the ground to seek the height from where she could look down and know where she was and see clearly when all the rest was gone.

WHAT SHE WISHED for—what she really wanted—was not to have to do anything. It wasn't that she was lazy and didn't want to get out of bed in the morning. She was not some heavy, inert woodchuck idling away in her little potting burrow. She just didn't want to do anything and remembered enough to understand that eccentric, misguided diversions taken up as remedies against boredom all contain boredom within themselves, are boring—Opa the Weimar polymath with his guppies and MAD magazines and never-completed book on Giambattista Vico. He had always been hard on people who he said lacked ambition. There was smart ambition and stupid ambition, and one had always to be critical, to distinguish between them. His Onkel Viktor, the "little bit famous" silent-movie actor, was always trotted out. He'd failed because the only thing worse than letting fame give you a big head was letting a little fame give you a big head. Onkel Victor died an alcoholic in the streets of Berlin in the winter of 1929 because he was "vain and lazy" and used difficult times as an excuse to let himself go. The only positive thing Opa ever said about him was that he'd been lucky enough to die before Hitler came to power.

But was it wrong to want only to live quietly and be left alone, to wish to come, all alone, through immensities? Maisie saw herself plummeting through thick banks of clouds, then slowing abruptly just above her house and as she touched down in her backyard glancing up through the towering clouds to see a castle turret perched on a mountaintop, reminding her of the great distance she had fallen and the greater miracle of her gentle landing. It wasn't terrifying at all but a comfort and reminder of starts and finishes and the amplitude of feeling that runs in a current between them—the thrill of giving up as much as the relief of coming down, of landing.

AN HOUR LATER she was back on the Garden State Parkway. She'd called before leaving. "Happy to see you, honey. Come by anytime."

"Will today be all right?"

"Sure, honey. Anytime you like."

She called again getting off at the Manahawkin exit, stopped at Walmart to buy flowers, and stuttered through the checkout line and back out through the outsized parking lot under scattered clouds and sunshine. Minutes later she pulled into Ocean Manor, parked in exactly the same space she'd parked in the last time.

But it was as if she'd never been there.

Sally was in the common room watching television with three other women and eating saltine crackers from a box. She was wearing the same print dress she'd been wearing when Maisie had left her ten days ago. She glanced up and offered the box of saltines. "Want one?"

Maisie squatted down in front of her and made eye contact. "Sally? Do you know who I am?"

Sally looked past her to the television, which was showing a nature documentary about Alaskan grizzlies. "Ever get black bears up by you?" she asked.

Maisie shook her head.

"Bobcats," a woman offered from across the room.

"Ever used a stopwatch?" Sally asked, munching a cracker.

Her attention wandered between the saltines and Maisie, who sat beside her, waiting and looking for cues and signs like a bus passenger uncertain of the next stop. Sally was calm, not addled or agitated and indifferent to the cracker crumbs collecting in her lap like fallen confetti. Maisie watched and waited for Sally to brush them away and, when she didn't, reached over and gently brushed them onto the floor herself. Sally glanced down, then back up at the movie. The next wave of crumbs fell and collected. Maisie observed now as if through a side mirror and couldn't say where she was anymore except someplace off Route 72 in a nursing home with somebody who had no idea who she was.

After a while Terry, the aide, came to fetch Sally, and they returned to her apartment. Maisie put the flowers in a vase. Sally was still preoccupied with grizzly bears and began telling a story of a notorious robber who had lived in a cave in an underground forest and threatened to burn people in their houses, "roast them like a pack of kittens." The side-mirror image continued receding to the horizon. It was no longer a real road. She was driving across a nameless, boundless grey plain. Maisie watched as Terry took her time attending—to what? She couldn't improve on it. Nor could she expand. Nor could she stay any longer.

As she drove back home, the signage flitted by, green placards addressed with place names like labels in a shop window. She could see each and every one at the center of its own hermetic everything, somehow connected in a way she could not grasp or imagine beyond roads and power lines and parking lots and minimalls and local news. Like Sally, a thereness and nothing more. A separate and separated thereness. It was also the only sense she had of herself, Maisie of Montclair via Riverside Drive who didn't belong to the world she'd grown up in. Neither Opa and Yva's Jewish Weimer old world or their old-world-made-new Upper West Side. Nor did she belong to Montclair, New Jersey, where she had spent most of her adult life, now divorced, a middle-aged woman living uneasily in a comfortable home that she could recede from anytime without leaving a trace. She was not lonely. But she was missing a place somehow. A connection. The rocks here matched the rocks across the Atlantic, where New Jersey and Africa were once joined. An exotic fact, a silly idyll Opa would have called tortured thinking wrapped around absolutely nothing. But Opa and Yva were also like those Triassic formations—not in the sense of primal origination points, just split between two continents with a world opened up between them.

OVER PATERSON MAISIE hit a pocket of dead air. Bump. A tingling began in her toes and spread to her feet. By the time she got home her right leg had gone numb, and it collapsed under her when she came down in the backyard, a little closer to the edge of the back patio than was comfortable or safe. She lay in the uncut grass, exhausted, not wanting to get up. Fibrous wisps of cirrus cloud drifted high in the jet stream. What stars shone through their yellowed haze twinkled in little patches. Though she couldn't see them clearly, she knew most of the constellations by name, a chart she carried in her head and navigated by. The December zenith: Cancer, Gemini, Auriga, Perseus, Andromeda, Pegasus—stick figures dancing in a line from east to west. Above and to the left, the upended dipper of Ursa Major pointed to Ursa Minor and Polaris, the North Star.

She rolled onto her side. The kitchen lights were off. Through the glass doors she could see the blue-green digits of the oven clock and the blinking red point of the motion detector and the alarm system they never used. It was cold, below freezing. She'd been out far longer than she'd planned. The house, silhouetted against the night, reflected a comforting moonlit glimmer. What if it rose up and moved off its foundation? Just a few feet to the right or left? Why not see a house the same way we see a butterfly? It was one of Alden's notes in the box. A succession of fixed postures, a discrete moment fixed Muybridgelike in time. A house alighting on the ground, flexing its wings for a time and gone the next instant. She wanted to take it in like that, the way Alden took in the cellar holes of Harrisville. She'd just flown over Paterson's white woven falls, dipped into Hinchliffe Stadium, fenced and condemned, sturdy weeds sprouting from the crumbling masonry and bleachers. She landed in the middle of the Art Deco amphitheater overlooking the falls, home of the Black Yankees, whom her father-in-law had seen play as a young boy. Then she lifted off again, circled the ruined stadium, banked, and followed the Passaic meandering like black glue through the engorged townships of northern New Jersey. Butterflies all, alight on the land, big things made way for, tiny things felt intensely.

Maisie heard voices, two figures coming up the driveway. She rolled flat onto her stomach, kept her head down, and watched as they crossed the back patio to the kitchen door. Heart thudding, she flattened herself, straining to look but afraid to lift her head. There were whispers, the sound of fumbling, and then a click and the whoosh of the glass doors sliding open. She lifted her head as the kitchen lights came on.

Of course. It was her son, Karl. Karl and his college friend. She watched as they moved about the kitchen, opened the refrigerator, turned on the counter lights. The friend was stocky, with a shaved head that gleamed in the halogen light. He looked like a wrestler. Maisie got up, brushed herself off, was about to go inside but stopped short at the edge of the patio and watched them through the doors. Karl's hair had grown out. He looked lean and shaggy. And he'd grown a beard! How changed he was. In just a few months. And handsome, too. Not just youthful but something else, something still hidden, yet to emerge.

She retreated into the shadows to watch her son, her only family. There had been no women, no siblings. Just surrogate parents and an unfinished child, a trouble to the peace.

"Mom! Where'd you come from?"

"You've grown a beard!" She went to him, arms outstretched, and hugged him warmly as the college friend came through with things from the car. "Let me look at you." She touched his fuzzy cheek with her hand.

"This is Dave, my roommate," he said, pulling back.

"Welcome," Maisie said and offered her hand, suddenly conscious of the figure she cut: staticky hair, reddened cheeks—a mother gnome in dirty jeans and running shoes. "You must be exhausted from all the driving."

"Mom makes pottery," Karl offered.

"That's awesome," Dave said, beaming, and nothing more.

They repaired to the kitchen. All were conscious of something new. If the college boys slouching at the kitchen counter with cans of beer felt a little forced and done in deference to some rite of passage, it was also immensely enjoyable and felt good and right to be playing along. Maisie made sandwiches and listened to Karl's account of an exasperatingly difficult professor, whom he pronounced with full freshman authority "a total asshole." She was pleased to see them devour the sandwiches, accepted the friend's compliment ("awesome") with the offer of another (declined), and sat with them at the kitchen counter with musing eyes.

The guest room, which Maisie had thought would be Karl's when Sally moved in, she had left unfinished. She resisted following them upstairs, curious though she was to see Karl's reaction to her refurbishments, the messy tracks of her abandoned plan. She cleared the counter and loaded the dishwasher. The house felt full again and big enough to absorb the sounds of her son and his friend talking cheerfully and banging around upstairs.

The beard, she could not get beyond the beard; or the snug fit of his shirt and the tautness he brought to everything—all the forms that had taken shape, filled out, become particular. It bothered her for some reason. She didn't know why. The bunched-up maleness was heavy and deeply lodged in him, as it was in most of Don's extended family, along with traces of Northern Jersey dialect and other *lwost reckids* of their belonging. She felt close to her son, understood him, but distances were opening up. Not estrangement but the raw otherness of adulthood. With the beard he looked joined in with something else, something new that would take him off in who knew what direction to who knew what purpose. Maybe it was merely growing up and generational, the ever-shifting gap that opened and moved like ice melt. Separate floes. Opa and Yva had been just as baffled by her. That had been a two-generation, double-divide made wider by culture and war and old/new world differences. Her son was of and from here, from Montclair, New Jersey. How had that happened? Undeniably it had. She saw it in the way he came downstairs with his friend the next morning and sat at the kitchen table thumbing their smart phones with the smell of coffee and sun streaming through the glass doors. It warmed her to see him so fully, so easily at home. For her there was always that remove, the sense of looking on, of being somehow elsewhere. Always somehow elsewhere.

Later that morning, after Dave had gone, Karl found her in the den. "What's all this stuff, Mom?" he asked.

"My father's papers."

"They look like plans for an invasion. You got them from the old lady?"

"From Sally, yes." She took off her reading glasses and passed him the photograph she'd placed in the center of the coffee table. "Your grandfather," she said.

"He was a hippie?"

"He wouldn't have called himself that. Anyway, he was too old."

Karl studied the photograph. Alden, striding atop a rock pile directly toward the camera. "How come you never showed me a picture of him before?"

"I never had one."

Karl eyed her skeptically. "That's kind of hard to believe."

"What's hard to believe?"

"That there aren't any pictures of your father."

"I didn't say there aren't any. Just that I never had one."

"Why not?"

Karl was sitting forward now, hands clasped, with his elbows on his knees. He reached for the photograph and examined it again, holding it flat in the palm of his hand. "How old do you think he is here?"

Thirty-one or -two, she wanted to say, but couldn't speak. She pursed her lips and shook her head as all the intervenient emotion bundled up deep inside her was loosened and began to quake.

"Mom," said Karl a little nervously, putting the photo aside. "Mom?" he repeated, finally coming to her side and sliding an arm across her shoulders. "It's okay, Mom," he said as she sat doubled over, eyes pressed hard into the heels of wordless, frameless loss.

"Forgetting has two sides," she found herself saying a while later. They were in the kitchen now, Karl having left the den to fetch a box of tissues and she having followed him, not wanting to seem too pathetic, in need of tending. He was uncomfortable. She could see him taking nervous measure, wanting to comfort but not sure how— and discomfited by his discomfort. The kitchen offered a measure of neutrality, which was also a relief to Maisie. She was astonished by the topsy-turvy clarity that now sparkled through her tears. Karl seemed also aware of an enhancement and slouched at the counter, waiting for her to continue. "Go on," he said.

When she didn't right away a measure of focus was lost. "A person forgets," she said at last, not fully clear what she was trying to say. "We all do. It's normal. We accept it. Then there is what and whom has been forgotten. That's a little harder to come to terms with."

"When you're the one who's been forgotten, you mean?"

"No. No!" she came back. "That's not at all what I mean!"

"What and who are we talking about, Mom? I'm not following."

"My father." She blew her nose. Clarity was slipping away. "Sally, too, I guess. It's about them, not me!"

"About you forgetting them?"

Maisie nodded.

"Well, they could be accused of the same thing, too. Forgetting you."

"No. They were pushed away. I was raised as if they never existed. We didn't have anything to do with them." She shook her head. "They didn't want me to forget my mother, though. She's the one whom I really have no memory of. There were pictures of her all over the apartment, so I remember her without having any memory of her at all."

"But you remember your father, even though you didn't have any pictures."

"I mostly forgot. It's complicated."

Karl stood up and slid his hands into his pockets. They wore their pants so stupidly low, she thought. He was great

at hurrying to the point. How quickly the window of interest glazed over and obscured mother-son intimacy. A little
was either not enough or too much.

"Sally thinks I burned down his studio, burned all his
paintings."

"What?"

"That's what she said."

His features were now a mix of surprise and skepticism.
He sat down again, keeping his hands in his pockets, coiled,
as if prepared to spring up and dash off. "Did you?"

"I don't think so. But I can't remember. Maybe I did."

He took this in, then went to stand by the patio door. "I
wouldn't obsess over it, Mom."

Did he want her not to think? Push everything off? She
didn't know how to respond. "I'm sorry," she said.

"There's no need to be sorry, Mom." He glanced at the
clock on the stove.

"You off somewhere?"

"No. Well, yeah. Not right away."

But she could see that he was. A separate cloud floating
across the sky, thoughts elsewhere; whether she shooed him
off or drew him into the details of her preoccupations made
little difference to the bigger picture. What was the bigger
picture? What more could she do for him? She didn't suppose much. He was glad to leave things as they were, would

prefer if she didn't tell him exactly what was on her mind, spell out all the reasons for her desolation. What mattered now was that they played their roles properly, which meant he was free to ask and she was free to answer. But ninety-nine percent of family contentment rested on those options remaining unexercised ninety-nine percent of the time, saving that one percent for negotiating the truly excruciating passages—and the little bursts of joy—that filled out the family story. Families, like lives, are mostly defined by what is never said and never accomplished. And so family stories endure mostly for what goes unsaid and what is never done. Even—and, perhaps especially—in happy families.

Maisie had done all she could. It was enough that she loved him, had brought him through to this point—in this room together on this day, neither of them knowing what to say or how much to tell the other. Maisie's long-buried feelings had little to do with here and now. Why should they matter to him?

An hour later he was gone again, and she was bent over a pot at the wheel, a favorite old Patti Smith CD playing in the background. It was warm in the studio. The kiln was cooling, a newly bisqued batch she was experimenting with and unsure what to do. She let go of the spinning clay, arched her back, and stood up. The rain had stopped, a tock tock tock of dripping water on mashed and fallen

November leaves. She took her phone and stepped into the damp twilight of the backyard for a breath of air.

"You're coming at Christmas?" Sally asked. "Isn't it already over?"

"No. Not this year."

"Will there be music?"

"Of course. What kind do you like?"

"I like all kinds."

"There's music everywhere during the holidays. We'll find a concert to go to someplace."

"The Sindia was filled with a million dollars in Christmas presents when it sank off Ocean City."

"The Sindia?"

"A four-masted schooner that belonged to John D. Rockefeller. It's buried in the sand between 16th and 17th Streets. A big, beautiful ship. A hundred and fifty yards from the beach. They all walked ashore. Nobody drowned. A million dollars was a lot of presents in 1901. We used to swim out there to look for them."

November light slanted through trees and whorling leafage. The temperature was dropping. Maisie was comforted by the convalescent feeling of the changing season, braced and gilded at the edges, her fingertips tingling with cold, phone to her ear.

"Sally? Are you there? Sally?"

No. She wasn't.

Maisie went back into the studio and resumed packing pots for the student-faculty sale. Her offerings this year were slimmer but more substantial, workwise, and showed a shift toward elemental forms. The complexities of earlier work had been replaced by simpler proportions, not just for example but for utility. She didn't care whether or not anybody bought her work anymore. It was liberating after all these years simply to sit at the wheel, to guide the clay with her hands and arms and back and the rotational forces of the spinning wheel, urging the unformed mass to find its center. To turn a lump of clay into a vessel. It was what she would have thought if she were thinking, which she wasn't, since whenever she did the center was lost and the wadded mass between her hands started to wobble and gyrate out of control. It wasn't thinking that kept it centered. It was feel. Touch. And as the clay was spun between her hands and took its shape—she would lose some portion of her own. She could feel it unfolding out of her, drawn and lifted like evaporating water, up, up into the air, then gathering into clouds to rain back down again toward the dark, spinning center. Yes. It was worthwhile in itself. Something she'd been doing for a long, long time.

four

Alden said there was quicksand in the dried-up bog behind his place and not to go there. Grandpa Pete had lost a cow in it once, had watched from solid ground as it sank down and disappeared, mooing helplessly. That happened long ago, but the place was still dangerous. Every time she flew over it Maisie imagined the poor struggling animal being sucked down into the earth, surprised in its slow cow way at how safe, solid ground could suddenly turn so viciously, cruelly soft, how a place could disappear and take you with it. She always swooped low to look for signs of sunken things in the barren patches where nothing grew. What was beneath those places? A giant chamber where swallowed things floated in darkness like guppies in a bowl?

After Sally left for work Maisie went out to the chicken coop to check for eggs. There were four. She apologized to the hens and visited with them for a while because it was going to be a hot day and the only thing worse than being outside on a hot summer day was being inside a chicken house. Her bike was propped up on the porch where Alden had put it before he left. If it hadn't been for the quicksand and the boredom, she'd have ridden out to join him. But she'd had enough of watching him sketch and make notes all day long. "What else is there to do?" he'd answered on the way home when she asked him why he was doing it. It reminded her of those horrible empty Saturday afternoons when the whole world was bustling around outside and she had nothing to do and nowhere to go and being alone in her room felt like a punishment. Why couldn't her father have been a doctor and cared for sick people? Or a businessman and sold things, or delivered people's mail, or drove a truck? Was he too weird for that? She thought of the Hasidic Jews down in the diamond district. Opa said they lived entirely elsewhere, but they seemed to belong just where they were and did their business in a way that seemed given to them and perfectly natural, if also a little secret. Would they have answered the way Alden had? Looked up at her from what they were doing, loupe screwed into one eye socket? What else is there to do? Could it be that for everyone there was one thing and nothing else, nothing better? Was that heaven? If it was, how would she ever find it?

She went to pick some flowers. Orchids grew everywhere in the bottomland. She knew where to look because Sally had shown her. Hidden in the milkweed at the edge of the swamp were sundews—roundleaf, which was common, and threadleaf, which wasn't. There was also Turk's cap lily—which really did look like an upside-down cap—and handsome Harry, which Sally told her not to pick because it was getting scarce. There was a little patch of it coming up near an old oak stump where someone had left a pile of rocks, probably old ballast stones hauled up from the river by someone wanting to build with them a long time ago. "There's no way to describe that special feeling you get when you stop and look at a flower. It's like stepping outside of yourself," Sally said. "Or passing in front of a mirror. You always see yourself when you stop and smell a flower. It doesn't have to be out in the woods. It can be a florist's shop or a church or a doctor's office. You stop. You smile. You bend and sniff. And you always see yourself stopping and bending and sniffing. Right?"

Maisie thought, yes, maybe. But wasn't sure. She wanted to see herself picking flowers the way Sally said she would. Looking down from some special place. It would be high up—but not too high. She would have to hover, but not for too long. Like a bee, come to think of it. Yes, that was it. A bee. Something very similar must happen when bees came upon a flower and hovered, stopped and sipped. Did they see themselves? How else would they know what to do and where to return to again and again and again?

It was warm and stuffy inside Alden's shuttered shack.

She set the jar of flowers she'd picked on his work table and propped the door open with a chair. He didn't have electricity. The shard of light stabbing through the entrance was barely enough to see by. She lit the kerosene lantern. Alden had taught her how to light it and how to adjust the wick so that it didn't smoke. She carried it over to the wooden rack along the wall where he stored his paintings. Holding the lantern up, she could see well enough to find what she was looking for and dragged it out and propped it against the wall. It was bigger than she remembered and just as unrecognizable. If Alden had told her it was the Avon Lady or the Virgin Mary instead of her mother—would things have turned out any differently? There were letters, but they didn't spell anything. And numbers and shapes and colors, which even in the gleam of kerosene light seemed muted and bright at the same time. Red and ocher. Yellow and blue. Brown and black lines formed themselves into hands that looked attached to arms; a face that belonged on a neck and shoulders. It was a woman's face, a pretty one, dressed like a queen and holding an electric iron. She had a halo around her head like something you'd see in a church. The longer Maisie stared, the less of all the details she saw and the more like her mother the whole painting began to look. It was Katherine. Her mother. Her mother of the photographs. Her mother in a short-sleeved blouse and belted skirt in Central Park. Her mother with Opa and Yva on a beach someplace. Her college-graduate mother, class of 1959. Her beautiful young mother, who had always been familiar and entirely a stranger.

She bit and peeled the cuticle on her middle finger, felt the creamy aftertaste of blood on her tongue. Plucking and peeling the little tab from the corner of the nail was an art and a pleasing distraction. She held the edge of the throbbing finger in her mouth and sucked until the blood taste was gone and the cuticle became soft and flappy and she could pull and twist until a stinging current shot straight from fingertip to wherever that place was that pain always tends to gather. She gritted her teeth and squeezed her finger tightly as the pain slowly dissolved. Maisie understood that Katherine's death had been too terrible to mention. Too painful for everyone; shooting and dissipating, like the pain in her fingertip, then throbbing for a long time afterward, all swollen up. She knew that Alden had been there. She could picture him quietly coming and going from Katherine's room at Mount Sinai and Opa and Yva following him with their eyes as they thought about what to do now with Maisie, their only grandchild.

She sat with her back against the wall and her legs straight out. The wood planks felt smooth and cool. The way the painting loomed in the semidarkness shot through by sunlight coming through the door reminded her of the silver-buckled shoes she had begged and begged Yva for. How beautiful they were on her feet. She could hardly take her eyes away as she walked in them. Each step she took in them made her happier.

It was hot with all the windows shuttered. The painting cast its own light into the room. In the lantern light it looked spectral.

"Slow down your thinking," Alden had said when he'd shown it to her. She tried it now and sat listening to a squirrel scampering in the magnolia tree on the side of the house. Birdcalls and the sound of an airplane winding away in the distance like a big toy. If it was possible to slow down thinking, maybe she could also slow down feeling. She held her finger in her lap. It began to throb. The kerosene lamp began to smoke. She turned down the wick and noticed how the dimmer, yellower flame made shadows in the thick paint. The surface of the canvas wasn't smooth but coarse and rough, a whole landscape of texture that she ran her fingers on, surprised at how hard and sharp the ridges felt. Alden must have made it to be touched like that. Maisie stepped away. What did he do all day with his sketch pads and maps? He'd shown her how to look through the alidade, all brass with shiny knobs that turned nicely and a compass and a bubble. She didn't know what she was supposed to see, and she asked questions that he answered as if he were someplace else entirely—or was at least trying very hard in his slowed-down mind to get there. "There. That's magnetic north." He rotated and clamped the table to fix it in position; then he bent to look through the brass tube. "No squares and grids out there," he said and tapped his temple. "They're in here. The idea is to get rid of them and still know where you are."

"Is that what you're doing?"

"Sort of."

"Why?"

"I want to put something there."

"Like what?"

"I don't know. Something big that can be seen from high above and far away. But first I need to look at the place in a different way."

"What way?"

"I don't know. As a container, maybe. Or a hole."

"A hole?"

Alden smiled and returned his attention to the alidade and the plane table. Maisie sat down on a fallen log where they'd set their things, not sure at all what Alden was telling her—except maybe just that he wanted to be left alone. The water on the bog shimmered in the warm breeze that began to blow. She picked up a stick and walked around the perimeter of their little encampment, poking around to find where hard ground stopped and sogginess began. After a while Alden stepped away from the instrument and waved his arm.

"Think of a hole not as something put in a place but something that is the place. An emptiness. What becomes a place more than a hole?"

She stopped poking with the stick. By the look on his face she could see that he was talking more to himself than to her. She stepped up to the edge of the table to see what he was drawing with his pencil.

"You want to put a hole here?"

"It's an idea."

"For people to come and look at?"

"Maybe just putting it here is enough."

"But why?"

"To work on the scale of nature," he said. "Maybe it isn't interesting to anyone but me. But right now it's all I have to offer."

Even with the door wide open the shack was heating up. It was hot and muggy, and there was nothing for her to do but wait and wait and wait. She wanted Alden to find her sitting there and to see himself seeing her the way Sally saw herself picking flowers. Now she wished she'd gone back to the bog with him. Not having a mother was supposed to be a sad thing, but she wasn't sad and couldn't even pretend to be. Yva was her mother, even though she wasn't, the same way that Alden was and wasn't her father and tadpoles were and weren't frogs and the torn cuticle of her throbbing finger was and wasn't hurting.

She left the picture propped up in semidarkness. She didn't want to snuff the flame or put the painting away. She wanted to leave it out and have it to come back to; to lead Alden there by the hand and see the look in his eyes when they entered and—surprise!—there she would be, no longer un-looked-at and forgotten but lit from below like something beautiful and special in a museum. It seemed the perfect way to show him she understood everything so that maybe he'd stop thinking about ruins and holes all the time and she could come and live with him and Sally.

THE VAPOROUS RIBBON of the Garden State Parkway unspooled below her. She tucked her chin to her chest and banked steeply, following an east-southeast bearing that took her over the causewayscape of the Amboys through the scrub-divided swirls of Middlesex and Monmouth Counties, where she picked up speed and began racing, an invisible speck moving over the landscape, like a satellite flashing briefly into view, then vanishing into something denser.

"Remind me who you are again?"

"Maisie. Alden's daughter."

"Ah, she was such a sweet little girl. And stubborn."

"Do you remember the fire, Sally?"

"Which fire?"

"That burned Alden's house down?"

"My Ronnie was a fireman."

"Do you remember the house fire?"

"Of course."

"Do you know what started it?"

"You're Alden's girl?"

"Yes."

"Well, then, you should know. Alden's girl started it."

"It was an accident."

"Yes, that's right."

"A kerosene lamp started it."

"Yes. That's right. Doesn't make much difference anymore."

"But it does, Sally. I want you to know. I left the lamp burning. But I didn't set the fire on purpose."

"Do you remember the '63 fire that started up to Mount Misery? Burned near two weeks and took out seventy-five thousand acres, practically the size of Philadelphia!" Sally settled back into her recliner. She pulled the grey shawl over her shoulder. "What was that movie about the bird?"

"You mean The Birds? Alfred Hitchcock?"

"No. About the seagull. Jonathan Livingston Seagull." She smiled. "He comes every day. Stupid movie. Even stupider book. Ronnie gave it to me for my birthday. I like the name, though."

The knot in Maisie's stomach tightened and loosened as she drifted in and out of Sally's recognition. Ocean Manor seemed dingier and more drained of life than it had just a month earlier. It wasn't the dreary weather. Why hadn't she noticed before?

"They're called gulls because of that," Sally said.

"Because of what?"

"What they do with their mouths. Opening and closing like they're gulping. They'll swallow anything. Seawater, garbage. What was that movie again?"

"Jonathan Livingston Seagull."

"The French Lieutenant's Woman! That was a movie!" The look on her face changed to something bordering on rapture.

"Maybe we can watch it together one day," Maisie offered, knowing she had to take the stones as they appeared in the stream and to step gingerly as they popped up from the depths, one after another. "I brought some drawings I'd like you to look at. From the box you gave me. A place I'd like to go and see."

There was no change in the look on Sally's face. She rubbed her knee. "Fire's important," she said. "Pitch pine, shortleaf pine, those trees can take fire. They burn quickly, then explode back to life, and the burned stumps send out shoots practically as the smoke is still clearing. Even oaks'll put out shoots and acorns from roots underground. No other trees can take fire the way the pines can. Over and over again. Same kind of forest has been growing here since the Ice Age."

A short while later they were driving west on Route 72. Sally was gazing quietly out the window. "It was his work," she said picking up the conversation as if there had been no interruption. "But even if it was still around and he was still around, the man and his work, who could say what was more valuable and which contained the other?"

Maisie took her foot from the gas and pulled to the side of the road. They sat for several minutes in the click click click of the emergency blinkers, buffeted by gusts of passing cars and trucks. It was very likely that Sally did not at that moment know or understand what she had just said. It had come to her. And was gone. Just like that. All Maisie wanted was for it to sink in.

In Chatsworth they paused briefly in front of Buzby's

store, now a gift shop for tourists. It was closed. There was nobody around. A vague memory of drinking Cokes through paper straws in the camper, Duchamp, was all Maisie could summon. Sally began talking about her years at the Ocean Spray receiving station and the bogs at Hog Wallow and the days of handpicking cranberries.

"Only do that with blueberries now. They were already wet-picking cranberries with machines ten years before I started working there. It was all floodgates and dams and mass production. But as kids we used to work the harvests. Long days combing the bushes with fingered scoops and filling wooden boxes. Then Mr. Haines started flooding his bogs and riding across them in one of those airboats like they have down in the Everglades. Whole families would come up and picnic on the dikes and watch Mr. Haines drive that boat across the flooded bog scooping up every last cranberry. Everything changed after that. I went to work in the receiving plant just down there. When I was a girl all I ever wanted was my own canoe. Or a sneakbox."

"What's a sneakbox?"

"A cross between a rowboat and a sailboat that you can take into shallow water."

"For picking cranberries?"

"No. For hunting."

"Did you hunt?"

"Me? No. A sneakbox is like a good pair of shoes that let you walk anywhere. Wetlands and marshes are like forests in the water. Dad knew all the coves and creeks around Little Egg Harbor, Great Bay, used to take us out there with him. It's a different world out in the marshes."

Maisie drove on, expecting to hear yet again how all had changed and all was gone. But Sally drew into herself and fell silent. Alden's diagrams and plans were spread out in the backseat. One was titled Jetport and Tomb. A statement typed on translucent onionskin was attached to it with a rusty paper clip:

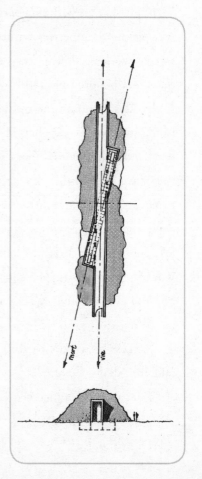

    Every airport is two different things. Seen from the ground it is a ramp, an avenue leading into the sky. From the air it is a portal leading back down to the earth, a refuge, a safe haven. The airport is the transition point between air and

ground where two modes of seeing meet, the aerial
and the terrestrial. These two modes of seeing
correspond to entirely different modes of being—if
being can be defined, at least in part, as spatial
existence—and to a particular perception of the
world as a consequence of travel and movement in
it. Created out of pure intelligence, an airport
is less a place than a situation, a straddling
of two dimensions, the terrestrial and the
aerial, where bodies, endowed with bird's-eye and
human's-eye view, are lifted from and descend
back to earth.

A tomb is all these, too. A transition place,
a point of contact between two worlds, the living
and the dead. Seen from above, it is a portal
into the ground, the site of return of the body
into the earth. On the view from below we can
only speculate. Nevertheless, the transition
from being to nonbeing can be portrayed as an
ascent into the heavens (as in Christianity) or a
descent into the underworld (as for the Egyptians
and the Greeks). The tomb, like the airport, is
the site of transport and transfer of the body
from one condition to another.

Sally began talking about water-skiing on the river and
a plan to build a NASCAR track up near Tuckerton—"Just
so you know that Jetport wasn't the last crazy thing people
wanted to stick here. Nobody remembers the racetrack that
used to be there. Got built when I was in high school by

some car-crazy boys who got together and cleared a place next to the town dump with axes and shovels and built the thing all by themselves. When they began racing their ho-trods people came from everywhere. Every Sunday more and more. The noise! You could hear it all the way down to Green Bank! And then Bob Dawson got killed the same weekend as Pete and Edie, and they shut the whole thing down, and that was the end of it."

"Pete and Edie?"

"Got run off the road on a Saturday night by some hot-rodder from Camden down here to race at the speed-way. On Hammonton Road near Wading River." She closed her eyes and shook her head. "Don't get me talking about racetracks, honey. If they build one, let 'em do it someplace else."

"Were Pete and Edie my grandparents, Sally?"

The question startled Maisie even as she asked it—that she had another set of grandparents, more people who belonged to another world, and her entire existence supported by all of them. Her Piney grandfather, whom she associated with sinking cows and ruined paper mills, she now could picture with Sally filling in the details of Pete back from World War II, a job in Vineland, a new car, and Sally's aunt Edie, who, when Pete was away at war, "took his gun and went out jump-shootin' ducks in winter when the marshes were frozen and the grass was all blown over in the wind and you could walk the meadows and didn't need waders or a boat. The men all belonged to gun clubs and had their blinds and their special spots all staked out, but Edie just went out there by herself and always shared the birds she took with us. Aunt Edie could dress and cook a duck! When Pete returned and saw what she could do with a gun he stopped going out with the boys and went gunning with her. People called her Double Trouble Edie—not because that's where she was from but because people didn't think a woman with a gun was anything but trouble. She kept her hair short so it didn't interfere with her shooting. Those days women wore their hair long, and Aunt Edie with her short curls sticking out from her hunting cap and the ducks she shot in a bag on her shoulder—that was something."

"When did it happen?"

She stopped to think for a minute. 1950. Or was it '51? And the picture sharpened into focus of Fords and Chevys and some tee-shirted, dungareed James Dean from Camden racing his oiled-up hot rod down Hammonton Road into a future none of them would ever see, all of it drawn by a concordance of real and imagined detail into something Maisie could see now for the first time. There it was. And wasn't. Spun from Sally's stories like fuzzy pink sugar on a stick, as insubstantial and delightful as cotton candy and just about as nourishing.

She wanted more, but Sally fell silent. Maisie touched her shoulder and slowed as they drove by the vast, empty cranberry bogs at Hog Wallow, where the pump houses were set like little red schoolhouses along the dike works all the way to the horizon. Sally kept her gaze fixed straight ahead, purse-lipped, jaw grinding gently. It was impossible to know whether she was lost thoughtlessly in the view or absorbed in some extreme obscurity of the past. Then she raised a bent, arthritic finger and pointed to a bird gliding over the bog. "Marsh hawk." She smiled, holding her finger up as if pinning the bird against the sky. Maisie leaned forward as the bird banked high over the car and disappeared behind them. She pulled over and stopped, and they sat for a time in silence, taking in the winter view. Sally kept her head turned toward the window as if speaking to no one in particular, not even herself, but simply recalling into existence things that had long been shadowing her mind.

"When they get their color a cranberry can handle frost down to twenty-eight degrees, but if they freeze they get all squishy. Flooding keeps 'em from freezing. They move the water from bog to bog. The smart growers do it by gravity; moving water uphill gets expensive." Her little bird scowl reminded Maisie of Yva, who could go around purse-faced for days.

"Did Alden know as much about everything as you do?"

Sally paused, as if the question were an interruption, then shook her head. "I was never sure what he had going on in that head of his."

"Did he know about cranberries?"

"You remember eating all those berries?"

"I remember chickens."

"Alden's girl was crazy about blueberries. I brought home a fresh box every day for her. Called her Blue Lips."

Maisie shook her head, unable to recall any of it, wondering whom she was being confused with. Or was it an orientation more than an actual memory, a figment of something that never happened? Little girls love blueberries. Little girls with blue lips are cute. Why shouldn't a sweet image like that become a memory? A little girl in an old woman's mind. She had no such memory of herself. But she did have others, and, few and scattered as they were, they were no more distinct than what Sally's memory offered and didn't displace Blue Lips as a figment of the past.

"Haineses' packing house used to be right here." Sally pointed to the Hog Wallow Road sign, and Maisie slowed as they passed by the empty intersection. "Burned to the ground one summer. I don't remember when. Went up in smoke just like that. A beautiful big old place, more like somebody's home than a berry-packing plant. We all drove up and cried and watched it burn. It was a huge fire. Ronnie was one of the firemen. Couldn't do anything about it. Just watched and cried."

They were on their way to another figment situated, according to Alden's notes, at the intersection of an abandoned crossroads to join the succession of non-places there, to mark and show it as coextensive with the physical world. It has now been mapped and emplaced and brought by these plans into being as a non-thing in a non-place. It is not meant to be a hallucination [L. hallucinator, hallucinate, to dream]. It is not false or distorted perception. It is not a delusion. It IS there: a massive, reinforced concrete slab six hundred feet wide that runs parallel to Iron Pipe Road, rising over the site of the "Ruin" at an angle of approx. forty-five degrees and breaking through the forest canopy to an elevation above sea level of approx. three hundred feet. If size determines an object, and scale determines art, the Jetport/Tomb operates on the scale of uncertainty. Its sole purpose is to function as a non-place in the same way the cartographic representation of the site on the USGS topographic map does. Whether it is ever built or not is immaterial.

"Tell me about your parents," Maisie said.

They had left the paved road and were now on a sandy track that led past the bogs into the forest. She drove slowly, recalling Duchamp, which had also felt sealed up, not the quiet cocoon of her BMW but a thudding box. Maisie tightened her grip on the wheel, steering between the parallel ruts in the road.

"Do you live in an apartment?" Sally asked her.

"No. I live in a house."

"I always wanted to live in an apartment. When I was little I thought only rich people lived in apartments. Houses were for poor folks."

"Do you miss your house?"

"Not much."

"You loved it there."

"Of course I did. But ... you can't dial back."

It was as if the car was driving itself, passing over an undulating gentleness that only seemed soft but, in fact, was more wearing to the car than hard turnpike asphalt.

"I didn't do anything wrong except put all of you out of my thoughts," Maisie said at last.

Their eyes met; then Sally resumed gazing out the window. It wasn't meant to be a confession but seemed to have been taken as one. Maisie frowned, let up slightly on the gas. She wanted to get back home, back to where she belonged. A real family, a real place, not some dark figment, some no place. They were now deep in the forest. Dense undergrowth brushed the windows and sides of the car. The track had narrowed; the sand was softer, finer. The wheels sank deeper, began to spin. She took her foot from the gas pedal, and the car came to an immediate stop. Nothing but green tunnel ahead and no room to turn around. To go back she'd have to drive out in reverse. Shit! She thumped the wheel with the heel of her hand.

"Are we stuck?" Sally asked.

Maisie stepped on the gas. The spinning wheels only sank deeper into the sand. Shit! Shit! Shit! She paused to collect herself. Then took a deep breath, pressed the pedal gently and let go, pressed gently and let go, rocking the car back and forth and feeling the engine and the wheels moving back and forth over the soft ground as if under the soles of her own feet. Then she stomped hard. The car lurched forward on a spume of flying sand, and they were moving again.

"Mountain laurel grows year-round," Sally said.

They were going downhill on a slight incline. The forest had thinned. The track widened, open to the sky above them. The straining of the engine in low gear was both encouraging and beyond nightmare. Maisie drove slowly, fully alert. All she wanted was to be out of there. The place.

The situation. The hide-and-seek they were playing, all the amnesia, age, dementia.

The track widened again, and they came into a clearing where jeeps and trucks had spun and dug their wheels, creating wide swaths and ruts in the white sand. Maisie stopped, but realized right away that the ground was too soft and the ruts too deep to turn around on. "Beautiful," she said acidly.

"Are we stuck?" Sally asked again.

Maisie got out of the car. They were on a shallow ridge from which she could see a good distance through the trees. It was not at all the flat topography of the map, which she spread out on the hood to study. Sally remained in the car, quietly waiting. The GPS showed them to be in a completely different location from where Alden's map showed them to be. How was that possible? She hadn't taken any turns. There had been no place to turn! She'd simply followed what appeared to be the main track. She got back in the car and fiddled with the GPS, which showed them as a pulsing blue dot against an iridescent field of green and no indication of a road. She took out her phone, trying to recall any turns or forks she may have taken—but there was no cell reception. Her hand was trembling. She was afraid, alert and alive, like something small and furry up on its haunches. An image came to her of the great treed pathways of Riverside Park in autumn, a tunnel of red and orange and yellow, the ground sloping gently upward on one side to the big stone wall and downward on the other to traffic and the flowing river. She could look up the steps at 103rd Street and see where she lived, the windows with the yellow drapes that blew out if Yva left them open, which she often did when the weather got cool and the air conditioners had been taken in for the winter. Maisie always paused at the bottom of those stairs. Then she'd zoom up in a wild burst that took her high over Riverside Drive, where she hovered and dangled, her little body securely knotted to that very certain place on the fifteenth floor, apartment 1519, her own intimate, familiar somewhere. You had to pass through so much clotted space to get there, through the bleeping, bleating city streets and avenues crammed with cars and people and architecture; through conspicuous places where people liked to gather as well as inconspicuous ones, little cracks, where a small child or a bum could hide and be left to shiver alone. She always zoomed up that staircase, flinging herself through inhabited space, because only in flinging and being flung did she know herself as something other than a piece of matter stuck and clinging like a pat of mud on a wall.

"Does your husband earn a pension?" Sally asked out the car window.

Maisie stepped over to face Sally. "He's not my husband anymore," she said. "And there's something else I want you to know. Something I want to show you. Watch me."

It was cold and silent but for the wind blowing through the wispy winter canopy of scrub oak and pine. Maisie walked a short distance up the dirt track and turned to look at the car, sleek and canted unevenly like a foreign object caught in the saturated underdrainage. Sally was just visible above the dashboard and seemed fully aware now of parting curtains and uncertain things to follow.

Maisie could feel the wet of the sand underneath her feet. It was all very vivid, the cold, the wet, the pearl-colored sky, the coming of evening. It pressed in on her from all sides—not gentle understanding, not happy surprise, not some tricked-out novelty, a flash—but a black and fervid temptation to rip something away, something that would change everything and could never be taken back. A breeze began to blow. Rather than flutter up on it, she began to rise, hotly, slowly. She wanted to put things into some sort of final, rational relief, all the great pains and little progress she had been busy with. But what she wanted was two things at the same time. Each had its own logic and justification and was right in its own way but canceled out the other. Her physics was all messed up. Maybe she didn't know where they were or where they were going. Maybe she wasn't a miraculous speck flashing against the sky but thick smoke billowing away in the distance; not something wonderful to behold, just something that would consume itself. She felt sudden resistance, a fluctuating current blocking her ascent, and saw that inside the car Sally was crying.

Maisie walked slowly back to the car, settled herself in, and took Sally's hand. She held on as the interior dewed up. Big drops coursed down Sally's cheeks. "I'm sorry," was all Maisie could say. "I'm so sorry." She squeezed Sally's hand, and they sat looking through the front windshield as if it were something they might leap through, holding hands, into some remote world they might never return from until Sally, at last, withdrew her hand, wiped her eyes on her sleeve.

"I thought you were going to leave me here," she stuttered with an embarrassed little smile. "Please don't ever do that again."

"I won't," Maisie said. "I promise." Then she started the car and, with three gentle rocks back and forth, pulled them out of the sand.

"JUST SIT DOWN there."

"What is it?"

"They're rocks."

"And mirrors."

"That's right. And we're going to need a lot more of them."

"Where do you get them?"

"A bathroom-supply place on Bowery."

"And the rocks?"

"That's harder. You have to hunt around."

"What's this one?"

"That's granitic gneiss from up near Pompton Lakes."

"And this?"

"It's all gneiss. Everything."

Alden's friend Sol came into the mostly empty third floor loft with another load from the camper, which was parked on 2nd Avenue right in front of the building. Alden was piling the rocks into containers spread out all over the floor of the loft. There were mounds of sand and rock salt with mirrors stuck into them. The grey light streaking through the windows at the front end of the enormous room and the bare bulbs hanging from the ceiling made it feel like a long, shallow cavern, a hideout. Sol and Alden were both sweating from hauling all the rocks up two flights of stairs. They looked like miners, all grimy and worn out from being too deep and too long underground. But Alden and Sol were enthusiastic, in high spirits, and worried only about being double-parked and getting a ticket before all the rocks were unloaded from Duchamp.

As he carefully stacked and piled, Alden explained how excavating raw matter from the earth with huge machines wasn't really much different from what people had been doing for thousands of years—think of Stonehenge—and whether you were using picks or shovels or dynamite, it was all organized wreckage, and there was a certain kind of beauty in the devastation caused in making a road or a building, which were also just organized piles of rocks. Sol, sipping a can of beer, described burying a box in a hole in Holland and something called a Portfolio of Piles that a friend was doing in Vancouver. That led Alden into a long description of Vista Rock in Central Park, the plans for which he had copied out of a book. He said Frederick Law Olmsted, the designer of the park, had moved ten million horse-cart loads of rock and dirt to make Central Park. Vista Rock, he said, was left behind when a four-thousand-mile glacier retreated north at the end of the Pleistocene and crushed and scraped and ripped the bedrock, forming what was the present-day Atlantic coast of North America. The city commissioners who hired Olmsted called Vista Rock an elephant and an eyesore because it cut at an angle into the Reservoir they wanted to build and prevented making it a perfect square. So Olmsted blasted a tunnel through it one hundred forty-six feet long, forty feet wide, and seventeen feet ten inches high and put the Belvedere on top—not just to please them or to make it more formal and picturesque but as a reaction to those old notions and to demonstrate his idea of a park as an ongoing relationship between people and a geographical, geological place.

Alden's face was flushed. What Maisie remembered best was not what he said but the sweaty contentment he exuded hauling those heavy crates of rocks, and his scuffed boots and dirty tee shirt and jeans and bare bulbs hanging from the ceiling and the indoor earthwork he was constructing as part of a long, involved conversation he was having with himself. When she saw the containers and piles again at Dawn Gallery (was it a week? a month later? she couldn't remember) it was as if she was seeing them for the first time.

The containers had been carefully made and filled with sand from places near Sally's house. There had been maps and mirrors and piles of dirt and other things she hadn't much thought about in decades except as details gone to seed in what were now flickering memories of her father.

Other details had gone to seed as well, which was why

she had never thought of him striding about the world in the glow of a rising reputation, an up-and-coming artist in the New York art scene. But he must have been all those things. So what about the rest? What was the real him all about? And all the high silence of forgetting and being forgotten that had been central to his vision and to what finally became of him? It was astonishing to think it had all been deliberate and conscious. And also troubling.

"WHAT'S YOUR CLEAREST memory of Alden?" she asked, stopping the car again and immediately regretting it.

"My best memory?"

"Your clearest."

"I don't know, honey. I suppose I don't have one."

"But you remember so much! What about everything you've been telling me?"

"That's different."

"Why? I don't understand."

"It all runs together."

"You don't have any favorite memories of Alden?"

"I remember when he brought his little girl to stay with me."

"That was me. You mean me."

"It doesn't make any difference whether it was you or not."

"Why do you say that?"

"Now, there, honey. Don't be upset."

Maisie stamped on the gas. It wasn't supposed to be like this. The track widened slightly and the ground firmed as they drove on, but the winter sunlight seemed thinner, less twined with the canopy, the trees, and the gaps in the shaded undergrowth. The sky was no longer the clear winter blue but had begun to grey over. There were only a few hours of daylight remaining, and the GPS in the dash still showed them as an isolated, blinking dot.

"Can you at least tell me more about how he died?"

"I don't know, honey. I wasn't there."

"But you went down there, didn't you? To claim the body?"

"There was nothing to claim. All we got was papers. Lots and lots of papers."

"Was he buried?"

"It was all too confusing. Just officials with stamps and papers." She fell silent and seemed to drift away for a time, then returned to Maisie.

Maisie continued steering through the parting brush.

"It was good not having a family," Sally said.

"Maybe that's why everything runs together," Maisie couldn't help muttering.

"And Ronnie. He was kind of a freebie."

"Freebie?"

"If you have nothing to give, you got nothing to lose."

"Well, the math works out, at least."

Sally resumed looking out the window.

"How can you remember everything you do and not remember Alden better?"

"I guess I just prefer not to."

The air between them had changed, but whether it had become more complex or had condensed into something simpler was hard to decide. Maisie didn't press the point, but she wondered if there were a difference between attachments we hurt in the absence of and love, which may be negated by too much attachment. But that seemed too abstract—a residue of truth-seeking reduced to utterances.

"You love this place," she offered at last.

Sally smiled. "Yes, I do, honey. I surely do."

Without warning, the screen in the car's dashboard flickered, and the field of green became a map again, populated by roads and features. In the same instant, as if somehow linked or tied together, the sandy track widened and became firmer, the ground flattened out, and the forest became less choked with undergrowth. A moment later they came to an expanse of open water, a marshland that stretched to the horizon. Maisie stopped the car and reached again for the map. Sally watched as she held it against the steering wheel and, tracing with her finger, tried to match it with the display in the dashboard.

"Penn Swamp," Sally said.

"But that's way over here." Maisie pointed to Alden's markings. "Unless we drove right by it."

"Used to be all lumber trails in here, every which way, going wherever the good wood was. They used to pack up their sawmills and move from one place to another. The whole operation. Take out the timber, mill it, and move on when pickings got too thin. My dad was in the lumber business for a while. Shuck crates and shingles. Imagine all that good cedar turned into fruit and vegetable crates. It was good business back then."

"Back when?"

"And decoys," Sally went on. "But decoys are made of white cedar. Red's no good. Know what a decoy is? A decoy is a coy duck. Dee-coy, coy duck."

Maisie glanced at her, then resumed looking at the map. Alden had put his Jetport/Tomb at an intersection where five roads came together. How had they missed it?

"And know what a swamp is?" Sally was saying. "An underground forest!"

Maisie considered the stagnant expanse choked with the skeletal remains of pine and oak, a dull, drowned world poking up from the muck. She was about to put away the map and drive on, but now Sally was biting her lip, struggling to control her emotions.

"Are you all right?"

Sally shook her head.

"Don't worry, I'm not going to leave you."

"Where do you live?"

"In Montclair."

"Montclair. Ronnie and I used to go to concerts there in summer."

"Brookdale Park! Don and I used to go to those concerts, too. We could have run into each other."

"There's lots of places to run into each other even if you never do," Sally said, turning away. The words hung for a moment. Maisie decided to drop it and resumed studying the map, tracing with her finger the road she thought they'd been on and landing on—Apple Pie Hill. Oh, what was the name of that raccoon? Rocky? No. That was the Beatles. The tune began in her head. Why did she remember that song better than the injured creature she and Alden had nursed back to health? Their wild pet. Was it all smashed pots? Shards pieced partially together? She recalled the ribbon of red taillights, the smell of asphalt and French fries. An open field with a collapsing barn and high-tension power lines beyond the fence where the camper was parked. The Turnpike and the Garden State were now wider and bursting with new tendrils so that the places they led to were hardly recognizable as the same places they once were and very possibly weren't, though Maisie didn't quite understand how that could be. It was too unclear to untangle or reason out. But there it was. A mysterious process of bonding and binding and breaking—place to place, person to person, person to place. She recalled the old folk tale of the phantom island that appeared off the coast of Ireland one calm day but disappeared each time the young men rowed out to it until, one day, an old man told them to shoot an arrow tipped with red-hot iron into it, which they did, and kept the island from vanishing under the water and made it habitable forever after. A memory fixed by burning arrows. The wounds heal and the shafts break off, but the iron tips remain. Embedded. What had they named that raccoon? She could see him waddling off into the night and remember being sad but not crying and being scared but not unhappy.

"And all these mirrors? Why are we putting them here?"

"They're holes," Alden said.

"Like the one you want to put in that bog?"

"Kind of, yes."

"Why?" She was confused and had wondered why he stopped to do this before taking her back home. She couldn't tell whether he was sad or angry. She had watched him as he photographed, turning the wheel on the Kodak Instamatic with his thumb after each snap.

Maisie glanced at her hands gripping the steering wheel, at her taut and stretched knuckles and the veins bulging on the backs of her hands. She turned to Sally, quiet now with her own hands in her lap, palms up, fingers laced.

Holes. Reflecting the light and sending it away, creating a void and turning the place into something else. Displacing, making a non-place. That's all that mirrors do. It seemed so simple now. She glanced into the rearview mirror, into the tree tunnel they'd just come through. After they'd propped the mirrors on the ground, piling dirt and sand at the base to embed each one in place, Alden had climbed a tree to take more pictures. There is something funny and also scary and sad about a man climbing a tree. Maisie wanted to climb too, but he told her to wait until he came down, and when he did, dirty and with hands all sticky, they sat down and looked at the work they'd done. The non-place they'd made. Alden hadn't said anything but just looked seriously at what they'd done, squinting through his thick black glasses, which he kept removing to wipe his sweaty brow with his forearm. Like in the bog, they had stayed way longer than Maisie wanted. She couldn't tell what he was thinking. The night on Apple Pie Hill had been the same. She didn't know if he was angry or sad for losing his job because of that damn raccoon. But maybe it hadn't been the raccoon's fault at all—maybe he'd lost everything for camping with an eight-year-old girl in the corner of a parking lot for days on end while he worked construction out on the turnpike.

"Oh, Sally," she groaned.

Sally turned to her.

But there was nothing more to say.

Maisie tossed the map back into the rear seat, feeling a sudden proximity to something she'd been unaware of, hadn't even known, just a few miles back. A sparrow can cling to a vertical brick surface—the exterior of a building—and stay almost indefinitely. She'd watched them from her bedroom. The little birds flew up from the park and attached themselves to the porous building surface by clinging with their tiny talons. They'd remain for a time, cocking their heads nervously this way and that like the movement of a small watch, then they'd relaunch themselves and dive back into the canopy over Riverside Park. What caused them to fly up into the vertical brick barrenness, leave the trees and crumb-strewn sidewalks to cling for a few precarious moments to the side of an enormous building? Was it an instinct to see how long they could be there? Were they escaping? Or was it simply to look back down at their home and what was familiar from a strange and distant vantage point?

"What in heaven's name are we doing here?" Sally said. "Nobody lives here!"

Maisie gestured to the plans and maps in the backseat, then stopped herself. "I guess we missed it."

"Nothing but grown-down ruins all the way to Atsion." Sally gestured out the window. "And Atsion's been grown down since before I was born. They put in the dam and the lake, and now Route 206 runs right through it, and nobody knows anymore or cares what's left and what's gone."

The car hit a bump, and, quite suddenly, the road became asphalt and they were out of the forest.

"I care," Maisie said.

And what she was about to add about what was left and what was gone, about all that mattered and all that didn't, dissolved in the glance that passed between them. She reached into Sally's lap and took her hand and held it. "Let's go home," she said and turned onto Route 206.

She was still holding Sally's hand on the turnpike as they passed the Molly Pitcher service area, speeding north in the brand-new express lanes and thinking of the fire tower on

Apple Pie Hill with views to the farthest horizon, of a little girl looking into a clear night sky and seeing an older
woman lost with all her maps in a forgotten geography of
the past. Why can't a woman who can fly also see her eight-
year-old self? Not asleep. Not dreaming. But alert and fully
awake. The child and the woman entire. The person she
thought she had forgotten and the person she had become.
It had to do with losing and finding something that hadn't
been missed—pennies beneath a seat cushion, Alden's
painting of her mother, love. It worked that way with flying, too; not just some trick of perspective at a distance but
placing herself in a universal space that gave her a single,
unique view. Love and the memory of it are always something different. But they are something. And always there,
somewhere, grown down with all the rest.

IT WAS LATE. And cold. Maisie was passing over the
Meadowlands and the I-280 interchange, hands stuffed in
the pocket of her flight jacket for warmth, mellow with
hope and the meditative mood of flight. At seven thousand
feet the arterial network of highways below cut this way
and that, radiant against clogged wetlands encrusted by
the flat, gridded polygons of commerce and industry. At
eight thousand feet the Meadowlands looks like a constrict-

ed heart, the oval, ventricular openings of the stadium and the racetrack discharging a coronal glow of orange-yellow light into the night sky. A small jet flashed up into the air from the asymmetrical X of the Teterboro Airport just to the north. She banked gently to the west to avoid it, trying to imagine the great slab of Alden's Jetport erupting out of the marshland, not the sparkling, vertical eruption of the Manhattan skyline, of human hands on the landscape, but jutting from the earth's crust at an angle only possible through the slow action of heavy tectonic forces: two different scales, human and geological, that each inspired different senses of contentedness and belonging. To feel at home in all that. To find a niche.

It was easier from up there, moving over the darkened landscape twinkling with lights. At altitude Maisie could be intimate on a scale of immensity, a singular emplacement over a profusion of places—the metropolitan sprawl, tens of millions of at-homes in repose on the earth below like ducks floating on the surface of a pond. Up here it was not one to one but one to many. It was the peace of altitude, of a universal space and a singular view, the peace of being somewhere and everywhere and nowhere all at once.

ACKNOWLEDGMENTS

I would like to acknowledge and thank the following for making my journey into the Pines so rich and rewarding. The works of Henry Carleton Beck, which are a unique and heartfelt documentation of the people and history of the region. John E. Pearce, a true historian of place and author of *Heart of the Pines*. Paul Hart and Jaclyn Stewart of the Tuckerton Seaport Museum, where traditions are not just on display but also passed on. Ron Spodofora, sneakbox builder and teacher extraordinaire. Carly Capelluzzo, for her love of wetlands and everything in them. Pete Stemmer, keeper of the Bass River History Blog. Ann Hoog of the Library of Congress Folklife Division. The late Nancy Holt, whose kind interest in this project served as both inspiration and benediction. Finally, my deepest thank-you to Patrick Basse, who shared with me his drawings and visions of place and whose memorial to Chloe captured my attention.